The Day OF KNOWING

A FUTURE STORY

Josh Moody

CentRed
PRESS

What Others are Saying About
The Day of Unknowing

Somewhere after Orwell's Ingsoc is Moody's dystopian vision of the future, *The Day of Knowing*. This totalitarian world with its nefarious use of the Internet leaves the door open, as all repressive systems must do, to the resisting human spirit. What happens next will keep readers engaged to the end. Moody's brisk story brims with ideas and a pathos that drives home truths that will linger long after.

THOMAS L. MARTIN
Clyde S. Kilby Professor of English
Wheaton College

With inspiration from Huxley, Orwell, and Rowling—along with a quick nod or two to Lewis—Josh Moody deftly creates a tech-driven, Big-Brother-landscape that is both unnerving and endlessly compelling. Devoid of books, free-thinking, and any semblance of faith, Josh's envisioned AI-enforced world presents readers with a series of unsettling glimpses of what could be, and how even the memory of the one true God can so-easily—and so quickly—fall victim to the man-centered digital voices that increasingly demand our attentions 24/7. A cautionary tale to be sure, but one that in the end points to the Living Word—and hope.

HAROLD B. SMITH
President Emeritus
Christianity Today Inc.

Josh Moody's *The Day of Knowing* transports readers to a vividly imagined future where echoes of a seemingly ancient past haunt a tightly controlled, technocratic society. At its core, this novel tells the gripping story of three brave friends who dare to challenge the mind control that dominates their world. With a narrative that is both engaging and humorous, Moody balances suspense and tension with moments of levity, making for a well-paced, enjoyable read. Moody skillfully employs symbolism throughout, contrasting the sterile, controlled environment of the present with mysterious influences from the past that inspire the protagonists to pursue freedom and independent thought. These symbols resonate with readers as a call to think critically and search for a higher good.

DYANNE K. MARTIN, PHD
Assistant Professor
English and Education
Senior Research Fellow, ISGAP

For Sophia

ISBN: 979-8-9906706-0-0

GodCenteredLife.org

Ep-i-ste-me, noun, "knowing"
(From Greek ἐπιστήμη)

CONTENTS

Chapter One

THE CATHEDRAL AWAKES 1

Chapter Two

FIRST DAY AT GAYLE COLLEGE 7

Chapter Three

FIRST CLASS 23

Chapter Four

THE COUNCIL 39

Chapter Five

DISAPPEARANCES AT GAYLE COLLEGE 57

Chapter Six

THE TRUTH 71

Chapter Seven

WIDER COUNCIL EFFECTS 87

Chapter Eight

ESCAPE..103

Chapter Nine

DESTINY..121

Chapter Ten

UNDERGROUND..139

Chapter Eleven

NEW BEGINNING..157

"Now does my project gather to a head:
My charms crack not; my spirits obey; and time
Goes upright with his carriage. How's the day?"

PROSPERO, ACT V., SCENE I., THE TEMPEST.

Chapter One

THE CATHEDRAL AWAKES

Rev. Style Modum was fast asleep dreaming of choir robes, choristers, and organ preludes, when a loud bang from the direction of the Cathedral woke him.

He greatly disliked being disturbed in the middle of the night, especially when he was in the middle of his favorite dream, but this noise was loud enough to interrupt even the most committed sleeper. He sat up, startled, scratched his head, rearranging the hair strands haphazardly across his bald scalp, and stumbled his way to the window that overlooked Durham Cathedral.

Much to his bemusement there was a light on inside the Cathedral, emanating from the end where the famous Celtic Saint St. Cuthbert's tomb was interred. The loud bang was repeated. Rev. Modum looked down at his watch, yawned expansively, and began to mutter to himself about 'student pranks' and 'it will be

1

the death of me and then they'll be sorry' and other such stolid reserves of the righteously grumpy.

As he made his way across to the Cathedral, clutching the keys to the medieval doors, Rev. Modum took a short cut across the grassy square in front of the Cathedral, aware that at that hour of the early morning no one would notice the break in proper protocol—nor his old running shoes poking out beneath his hastily arranged cassock which he had thrown over his pyjamas as the easiest way to get dressed. The mist lay thick like porridge; there was no moon.

Still, the Cathedral itself, with its surprising light at the end, appeared like a sleeping dragon, one eye awake, watching cautiously, while around it all dozed.

As the door to the Cathedral creaked open, Rev. Modum was relieved to hear no other bang, nor scuttle of feet of the alarmed in the midst of some heinous crime or unworthy student joke at the expense of the clerical establishment. In fact, if the light at the end from St Cuthbert's tomb was not still shining all would have appeared entirely normal—at least for that time of the night. Usually during the day there were visitors, and tourists, and the intermittent sparsely attended service. The Cathedral was quiet, *exactly as it should be then, he thought, except for that d___ light.*

He bit back the expletive; "Dratted I mean," he said, looking around at all the religious symbolism that his handheld torch picked out from the walls as he trotted down to see St. Cuthbert.

Cuthbert's tomb had a strange history, he knew.

Legend had it then when it was first dug up Cuthbert was discovered inside entirely without decay; a miracle, they said at the time, and this gave the tomb of St. Cuthbert a caché in the Middle Ages which he had never entirely lost. A later excavation revealed a book, in fact the oldest book discovered in England. People came to see the tomb still, hoping if not for a miracle at least for some ethereal, other worldly, sense of timelessness that such ancient monuments yet have the power to enchant.

The Cathedral was now deathly quiet, as if the entity that was the Cathedral somehow held its breath waiting for a great new discovery around Cuthbert, or was nervously keeping its breathing to a minimum so it would not be overheard while it watched from the shadows what was about to unfold. Rev. Modum had the habit of thinking of the Cathedral as alive, a habit he had never quite admitted to himself, let alone to anyone else. His heart beat noisily, and his breathing increased as he rounded the corner to where St. Cuthbert's remains lay; he could not quite decide whether the Cathedral was watching uneasily, expectantly, or hopefully. As the thought came to his head, he pushed it to one side; "Bricks and stones," he muttered, "bricks and stones."

On the floor next to Cuthbert was a lamp, the likes of which Rev. Modum had never seen before. It was brighter than he anticipated, from such a small object, and the light shone with a clarity and intensity of which he was not familiar. As he bent down beneath its main beam of light, and inspected the lamp a little more closely, he noticed that it was twisted round and round like the outside of a miniature version of the slides you see at fairs. Except there were two interlocking sets of slides, one running in one direction and the other in the alternative direction: like a double helix, Modum mumbled to himself, remembering his genetic lessons when as a student he had heard of the discovery of the shape of DNA by Watson and Crick.

Staring at this light, and the oddly shaped lamp from which the light shone, Rev. Modum stood up and slowly began to glance around the area to see if there was anything else unusual. It was then that he noticed that the tomb itself was rent open—cracked, and broken with a vast aperture through which it would be easy to place a large object, or remove one.

He gasped. That tomb had not been opened for hundreds of years, and yet now it lay rent and ripped halfway across its expanse, with a jagged edge as if it had been cracked and then torn, or peeled like an egg.

"That must have been the reason for the noise," Rev. Modum said in a half whisper, "those students have gone too far this time," he added, louder now as he began to feel incensed at the violation of Cuthbert.

He would need to call the police, he knew. "Drat and Bother," he said; "Drat and Bother."

He had not brought his phone with him so he would have to go back to make the call, but before he left the scene of, what he now called, "the crime," he could not resist taking a peek inside the tomb itself.

What would be left of Cuthbert, he wondered?

The light shone eerily past the opening, casting a faint glow inside the hole itself so that if he was careful he would be able to make out at least part of what was inside without unsettling anything, or fudging any finger prints that the police might need to discover.

Once more he bent down, this time not by the lamp but by the opening to the tomb. *Strange*, Rev. Modum said to himself, *that a man so long dead should still carry such fascination—and cause so much bother.* As he looked inside the tomb, he noticed the light shone not on a body, or skeletal remains at this point in the opening, but on what at first looked like a parcel.

Using the hem of his cassock, not to leave any finger prints himself, he reached in and picked it up. He put it on the cold beating floor of the breathing Cathedral.

It was not a parcel, it was a manuscript, ten folios or leaves of parchment, he counted in all.

On the front was a date in Roman numerals. Rev. Modum stared at the date long and hard. He blinked hoping that the obviously, or apparently, ancient manuscript would reveal a different claimed date if he looked long and hard enough at it. Or if he shut his eyes briefly it would go back to revealing a date that would make more sense to his tired, sleep-filled, eyes.

"*MML.*" That could not be right, he said to himself.

And yet there it was blinking back at him each time he blinked his eyes at it, like some strange apparition from the future. He remembered his Latin well enough to know what the date said, and yet how could it mean what it said? The parchment was clearly old, and yet it spoke of a time still far in Modum's future. He turned over the ten folios of parchment one after the other and began to translate the story he found.

"The year 2050," it began. "The Day of Episteme."

Chapter Two

FIRST DAY AT GAYLE COLLEGE

"John," the voice floated across to him from the car.

It was the first day at Gayle College, and all the steps up to the iconic old campus main entrance were crammed with new students buzzing around like so many bees in search of nectar. They were looking each other up and down—the men eyeing the women, the women the men—sizing one another up to begin the process of discovering their place in the university hive that they were joining.

Who were the sporty "jock" types? Who were the intellectual "nerds"? Who were the beautiful people—and who the outcasts?

"John," the voice came again. It was his mother.

Smirks began to be formed on the lips of his fellow first year students, who began to look towards him the way that passersby on highways stare at car accidents, unable to restrain their curiosity.

Just how bad would this be, you could see they were wondering. *He has his mother calling to him. Did he forget his diapers? Does he need a last kiss from mummy to help him not feel homesick and cry himself to sleep tonight?*

John Broadus made his way slowly back down the steps to the family car. Like all cars in 2050 it had been fitted with mind controls, so that when connection was made by hand to the terminal at the front of the car the controls were operated by thought, though it was rather out of date and had nowhere near the same precision of operation as the latest "mind rovers" which could go off the highway grid as all terrain vehicles.

His father was sitting in the driver's seat, and he now disengaged his hand from the thought pad while he waited for his son John to respond to his mother's calls. Mr. Broadus was of sufficient girth that he hardly needed to lean forward to touch the thought pad, though it was hard for him to squeeze his ample frame into the seats at the front of the car. His puffy eyes rolled as he noticed John's embarrassment.

Finally John arrived. "Don't speak so loud, Mother," for some reason John always used the formal sounding 'mother' and 'father' when addressing his parents—more intimate expressions seemed strange to their relationship, as if there was a hidden distance between them despite the closeness that you would expect between an only child and his parents. Even when they were physically close it always felt to John as if they were talking across a barrier, not like people in the same room but neighbors discussing the weather across the neighborhood fence.

He glanced behind him; most of the students were now looking elsewhere, their attention captured by a first year who was wearing the latest most fashionable this-year-hat, a rainbow rendition whose colors reflected the mood of the wearer (if he or she so wished), or could be projected to reflect the colors that the wearer wanted others to see and think that they were feeling. He had never had such "fashist" fashion himself, his parents dressing him in what they perceived were sensible clothes, but were really sensibly inexpensive to their pocket books.

"John, I want you to call us each day."

His mother was the kind of person who liked to know what was going on all the time without delay, in dependable and frequent downloads of information. She did not like to be kept waiting, and she would be insisting, John knew, in a moment that he call her up at set times of the day—this was going to be impossible if he was to actually try to enjoy himself at Gayle College. Besides, he did not want to have to call her every day.

"It's only fair," she said.

Ah yes, that well-worn trump card: guilt. John was an only child, his parents had told him, because being originally a twin his sibling had died in utero, a failure to thrive inside the womb, and the impression that John had been given was that it was because he had used up more than his fair share of resources. Now, 'it was only fair' that he play the part of at least two children for ever since the miscarriage of his sister, he was told, his mother had been unable to have any more children.

John sighed. He had never found a way to counteract the trump card. "I will do my best," playing the dutiful son; but honesty compelled him to add, "but I cannot promise. You might have to get used to only hearing from me now and then." John was thinking it would be more then than now, occasional at best certainly not frequent.

His mother did not smile back, she knew her son well enough to realize that his response was not exactly fulsome, and too non-committal for her taste. But she did not look particularly disappointed either; as they continued to linger by the roadside of the entrance to Gayle College, John's grand entrance to his first year had already been marked by her extended presence in a way that he would not have wished, and she longed for. Something in that gave her satisfaction, even if deep down she knew that she would rarely be hearing from him from now on. She wanted him to be reminded of her presence, of her influence, and to have inserted her wiry, some would say skinny, frame into his mind at this psychologically important moment was a victory of sorts.

This was all instinctive to her: all she knew was that, as the students around John periodically stared at him talking to his parents at this awkward moment, even as he left her he had not entirely escaped. After all, she reasoned, there were dangers everywhere, and while Gayle College might be safe for now from The Contagion, nowhere was safe, and it was better that he have a motherly anchor as security if there were a storm.

John made his way once more up the steps to Gayle College, without a backwards glance, and joined the throng of first year students wandering about, exchanging nervous grins and what they took to be witty repartee but was more like canine sniffing greeting rituals than exemplary higher reasoning. Gayle College was a remarkable place: its towering pinnacles, its ancient brick façade, its stone interiors masking cold flagstones and secret passageways to explore. Gayle College loved its secrets, the hidden rituals, the special school song, the secret societies known to all but whose members were known only to each other.

"Nightmare!" a big smile joined the empathetic description of what John had just been through.

"I saw it all!" she said, "I don't know how you put up with it. If that had been my parents I would have disowned them on the spot. You must be nice."

The word 'nice' was half compliment, half question; it came across as a tease.

"Or just plain dumb!" this from another student, a man like John, who was running up to greet him too.

"Ignore him," said the girl. "By the way, my name is Emily," she said, "Emily Lee."

"If you had said it the other way around it would have had more impact. You know, 'my name is *Lee*. Emily Lee.' Like the old Bond movies."

"Oh do be sensible," said Emily. "How old are those movies now? Next you'll be quoting me Shakespeare or something."

"Who?"

"Never you mind," Emily quickly added, noticing the surprised look on John's face at the mention of someone whose works were first written in actual books, even if they were only accessible now through the Webispace, the ever present data source that everyone used nowadays instead of books.

"By the way," said Emily, "this goon here is called Jimmy. He's not half as tough as he looks."

That would not mean that much because while Jimmy at once burst into an appreciative gleaming grin directed at John, he smiled down from well over 6 feet 5 inches, and the hand that he extended towards John was as large as a midsized frisbi—the mind controlled discs that were now zipping around the campus according to their individualized users instructions, sometimes expertly sometimes careering ludicrously out of control.

"Actually, it's Cowan. Jimmy Cowan." He laughed along with the smile.

Seeing the two of them stand next to each other made John start to feel a little better that first day at Gayle. Jimmy was enormous and beaming, reassuringly strong looking, in a mildly scary way. Emily, by contrast, was petite, and, John noticed, nicely shaped. The word 'nice' popped back into his mind in an unexpected way as he shook her hand.

"It's time," said Jimmy, "for the Great Hall."

"What?" said John. "What's that?"

"Don't you know what's coming next? It's tradition. Every incoming class parades into the Great Hall to be inspected by the students two years ahead of them, and then has to listen to a speech from the Dean of Students."

"Or the President," said Emily.

"Or the President," agreed Jimmy.

"How come you two know so much about it?" John asked them.

"How come you don't know anything about it?" Emily replied. "Everyone has heard of the Great Hall speech."

"I haven't. I am the first in my family to come to Gayle College."

Emily and Jimmy looked at each other. "You're a firster?" said Jimmy. "Wow. There won't be too many of you around today."

"What do you mean?"

"My parents came here before me," said Emily.

"So did mine," said Jimmy.

"You see," said Jimmy, "firsters are dead rare nowadays. Ever since The Contagion began, New Angle Land has tried to limit those who are given knowledge to families it knows are safe."

"Or thinks are safe," said Emily.

The Great Hall did not disappoint. Its rafters were high above the oak tables beneath, tables which were worn glassy smooth by countless elbows over almost a millennium in which the Hall had stood, though the actual tables were merely a hundred years old or so. There were medieval tapestries on the walls, festooned with flying animals, strange magical beasts, dragons, unicorns, as well as the equally strange now extinct beings, lions, tigers, and leopards.

Gayle College was a small elite school. It was much smaller than in its glory days, now numbering only a couple of hundred or so in each year, which meant that all of the undergraduate classes could squeeze into the Great Hall for the traditional first years speech. There was no head table, as such, but a series of interlocking tables, one with the other, arranged to emphasize that while there was some gradation of rank—and year—and the faculty were distinct from the students, still, all being said, they were all part of one fellowship of Gayle.

John Broadus put himself down at the nearest corner, where he hoped to be inconspicuous, and Emily and Jimmy sat down next to him. Soon the tables began to fill, so that there was not a spare seat in the whole room. It was a very large hall, but with all the classes gathered for the traditional Great Hall speech at the start of the year, there was not a space to be found left empty at all. The faculty were seated at one end, clearly senior, but not still different in absolute terms, if different in rank, wearing their faculty gowns, and talking intellectually (John assumed) about various high powered matters of the mind.

Before John could think much about this, or indeed engage in any scintillating conversation with those around him, the well trained waiters brought out course after course of food. To be honest, when compared to times gone by, the meal was nothing to write home about. It still came out served on best china, and the utensils were still for this meal at least the gold cutlery that had belonged to Gayle College for many a year. There were several different courses—fish, first, then meat, then a palate cleanser, then dessert, then cheese— but while all the rudiments were there the actual food did not taste as it used to. At least, that is what the faculty said each year, talking about the food, in fact, not about their classes, or their latest experiments in the laboratory.

To make up for the food was the drink. Not enough was served to make anyone tipsy, but the quality (not the quantity) was simply incredible. John had never tasted anything like. Best claret, served after having sipped genuine champagne, and after all was said and done came port, to be passed, John noticed carefully, to his left, and then lastly brandy. There were no cigars (like in the old days) but the wine was still from the old wine cellar, somewhere in the catacombs beneath the Great Hall, and it was of superior quality.

There were occasional remarks here and there between the students as they ate—a 'how are you doing?' or a 'pass the salt' or 'wow that tastes good', as a glass of wine was studiously sipped, but extended introductions were put on hold while the food, and the drink, passed from bottle to glass, from plate to fork to lip. Soon, though, once more the hubbub of conversation surfaced above the clink of knife and fork, and John began to look with interest about him. Sitting diagonally opposite him was a brunette, whose eyes twinkled with amusement as soon as he looked in her direction.

"Hi!" she said, "I think you liked the food! I don't think your eyes have risen above the level of the cups and plates in front of you for the last ten minutes!"

If anyone else had said it, John might have taken offence, but there was something about this speaker, a certain guileless charm, which begrudged annoyance and seemed to guarantee good humour.

"Well, it's good to meet you too!" said John smiling back. "My name is John. Who are you?"

"I'm Faith," she said, "Faith Felicity. Who are these friends of yours?" she asked, pointing towards Emily and Jimmy. John introduced them to Faith, pleased that someone might so quickly assume that they were friends after they had only met an hour or so ago at most. *How time flies*, he thought, *at Gayle College*.

"This," Faith said after she had expressed her happiness at meeting John's friends, "is Labelle Malchance." She pointed to the person sitting next to her. John could not believe it had taken him this long to notice her. His mouth would have fallen open if he had not been in the middle of taking a sip from his port glass. She was, he thought at that moment, simply the most beautiful thing he had ever seen. Her hair was golden, an almost white blond which fell in sheets like rivers to her shoulders, where they bounced in perfectly formed curls. Her eyes were large pools of welcome, which suggested invitation with every blink of the long eyelashes above. Her mouth, opened now to say how pleased she was to meet John, seemed to speak succulence even as she said simple things like, 'I am pleased to meet you' and 'where are you from?' Her lips moved against each other like long legs longing for some exercise.

John shifted uncomfortably in his seat as he tried to speak the normal polite phrases while his mind was still racing at meeting such a rare sight; as he talked he noticed that Faith was looking at him with a mixture of bemusement, and sisterly protectiveness. Evidently, Faith was not immediately drawn to Labelle Malchance in the way that most men would be, and wanted to communicate to John, to whom she already felt some family-like kinship and loyalty, her fealty and her unease at his immediate responsiveness to Labelle. She did not look suspicious of Labelle, certainly not wary, but she seemed to have formed a fairly quick three-dimensional view of her, which did not discount her qualities, even the more obvious ones to the observant eyes around, but weighed in the balance with a more mature judgment.

"And this," Faith carried on, interrupting John's extended glance between broken pieces of uncomfortable conversation with Labelle Malchance, "is John!" She smiled. "It's going to get confusing, isn't it? His full name is, well why don't you tell him, John?" she suggested, looking now at the person on other side to her, a midsize man with thick glasses, an introspective air, and what looked like soon to be wrinkle lines of concentration already formed at the corners of his eyes, crow's-feet of intensity and focus.

"It's John H. Johnson."

"What does the 'H' stand for?" asked John Broadus.

"It doesn't. It's just 'H'. I don't know, I guess my parents just decided that it sounded good and put it in there for effect.

Make me seem more sophisticated to the folks around, I suppose." John H. Johnson said it flatly, matter-of-fact, without any sense of astonishment. It was just the way it was, he seemed to be saying.

"Well," said Emily, joining in the conversation now after she had been talking to Jimmy for a little while about the best way to throw a frisbi, "I think we should call you H. It will keep things simpler if we're all going to get along together."

"Who says we're going to get along?" said Labelle Malchance.

"H. will be fine," H said, though without enthusiasm. "I've been called far worse in my time I can tell you that at least."

"Shhh," said Emily, "I think that's the president about to get ready to make the Great Hall speech."

"It's the Dean," said Faith and Jimmy together.

"No," said H., "it's Gary E. Dreyfus. His "E" stands for Edwards. He's the president. He's famous."

"To a 'nerd' maybe," said Jimmy.

"Or infamous," said Faith, smiling at Jimmy. "Did you hear how he got the job in the first place? Nasty piece of work from what I hear."

"What?" said Labelle, incredulously.

"Shhh," said Emily.

"Ladies and gentlemen," Dr. Dreyfus began. He was a surprisingly small man, standing unimposingly on a block put for the purpose behind the lectern to raise him to the height he needed to be seen by those around him. He wore a gown, black, with green down the sleeves, and a mortarboard hat. It was said that he preferred the hat because it gave him extra inches. Small he might be, but his voice was large, sonorous, and arresting. It was not sweet, but it was powerful, like a truck engine roaring, his words punctuated with precision like a hammer on soft wood.

"Ladies and Gentlemen, as you know our country of New Angle Land has risen from the greatest crisis that faced Western society by a simple expedient, radically applied, without sentiment, or fear of favour or recompense. When to our fathers it became obvious that the cause of extremism and violence in our world was the expression of religious opinions publicly, they banded together to ensure that, step-by-step, such expressions of religious devotion, inevitably extreme in one way or another, were hence forward to be blocked from every street and thoroughfare. In their wisdom they realized that in the heart of many an uneducated individual would inevitably remain a desire for some mysterious connection with a deity, or god of some kind or sort, so they did not even attempt to argue against such base instincts, or what some of the old religions called natural senses. In our own private selves we are free, as always we have been, to believe as we desire, though I trust none at Gayle College will be taken in even in their own private thoughts by the wild claims of yesterday's religious devotees.

"Yet outwardly, publicly, all religious expressions were removed, without sentiment, or fear of tradition, or effect. And the result was marvellous!"

Faith grimaced behind her hand at John Broadus. "Yeah, right," she whispered, "Marvellous if you are on the right side and toe the party line and don't mind what happened to everyone who doesn't agree!"

"We have unbroken years of peace!" Gary E. Dreyfus continued, unaware of Faith's whispered disagreement.

"Huh!" Faith said even quieter, whispering once more behind her hand, pretending to scratch her cheek. The President carried on regardless of any in the audience who might consider otherwise.

"We have not been disturbed by religious extremism once in the years following. Our old cathedrals have been put to more practical use, our chapels serve the economy, not the fantasies of addled brains, and the church in any institutional sense of the word for all intents and purposes no longer exists."

He looked around the room. Despite his stature, his words amounted to much, and there was a resounding silence that greeted his rhetoric, and his summary of the impressiveness of the solution that New Angle Land had found.

"Now my friends," he dropped his tone somewhat as he smiled briefly at the students, as if acknowledging that however strictly inaccurate 'friends' might be as a description of his relationship to them, it was a token expression of affection that he magnanimously dispensed. "Now my friends, you are here as the best and brightest of your generation. In the wars of religion which still live in our recent memory, many great men and women were killed, the flower of their age, the glory of New Angle Land, the hope of the future. You, and your descendants after you as before you, sit in their place, drink from their cups, eat from their plates, and must fill up to the brim the responsibility that is yours to make this next generation ever less 'religioned' and ever more free and prosperous.

"I speak to you now frankly, for this Great Hall speech has a long tradition of such openness in the fellowship we enjoy at Gayle College, and only to confirm what some of you have heard. There is a new Contagion, a virus of the mind, that is threatening our greatest achievements, and it will be defeated, and you will play your part as you learn at this august institution to think clearly, and to always—always, mind—accent the positive, the very positive.

Enough of such duties. Tonight we celebrate. We have a new class at Gayle College. Our ranks, though smaller than before, our healthier than ever, and though there is a cloud on the horizon, we in our fellowship will stand strong."

With the traditional ending to the speech the ranks of Gayle College, undergraduates and faculty, pushed back their chairs and with a rattling chorus stood to their feet. As the violins, placed in the corner earlier in the meal for this moment, now began to play the tune to Gayle College's song, the Fellowship Cup began to be passed.

Inside it was a mixture of rosé wine, watered and weak, mixed with spices and herbs, a white cloth around each handle of the ancient large cup, and slowly, slowly it was passed down the rows of the students and faculty. "Gayle College," one said, as he or she faced the other and passed the cup while the old silver lid was held by the one who did not drink, a gulp, a quick sip of the Fellowship Cup, a bow of the head to the Fellow of Gayle College standing opposite, and the same drama was repeated around the whole room, while the music of the Gayle College Song was played.

Together we stand as one
Facing each other we are strong
We have now no need for God
Our fellowship is our mighty rod
And we can do no wrong

John Broadus followed the others, aware of the famous song, if not the secret ritual of Gayle College before tonight, nor the fact that the words had been changed to fit the same tune with the new message of New Angle Land. The bow, the cup, the quick gulp of spiced wine, all the time the violins playing the music to the well known words of the Fellowship.

"Well," said Emily to John Broadus as they began to file out of the Great Hall, "that was an eye-opener."

"What was?" said John.

"He lifted the lid on The Contagion. He talked openly about it. Apparently we are part of the solution."

"What's the Contagion again?" said John.

"Firsters!" Jimmy slapped John on the back as he went by, "Don't you love them!"

Chapter Three

FIRST CLASS

John Broadus awoke to an alarm going off in his head. Unlike the Great Hall, the rest of the rooms, and classes, at Gayle College were all connected to the Webispace—the ubiquitous mind web which delivered information, pictures, and in this instance early morning wake up calls.

You could disconnect from the Webispace by removing your hand from a thought pad, or, as John now did, standing up and removing his body from his bed which was also connected to the Webispace. But most places were now thankfully wired into the Webispace and to disconnect would cause surprise, if not consternation, reported back through the "Walkers," the drones who monitored the Webispace at all hours of the day and night. Except for traditional rooms like the Great Hall where the old fashioned structure, and the history and culture, meant that as yet there were no thought pads, and no Webispace communication.

As John leapt out of bed, enthusiastic even at this hour in the morning, he was immediately aware that it was first day of classes at Gayle College. He had been looking forward to this moment for the last several years, and having managed to be selected for the elite group of Gayle College undergraduates, he was keen, even though he felt lousy this morning, to try to make the most of it all. That at least meant being on time for his first class. John stepped into the shower, taking with him the early morning coffee which he had ordered mentally immediately on waking, and had been delivered to him through the in-room catering that was sometimes used by students for breakfast—at least. He might be enthusiastic for his first class, but if he could avoid breakfast with everyone else that would be great.

John dressed himself in what he took to be passably fashionable clothes. He had none of the latest "fashist" black boots, and black jeans and top; his clothes were in any case, though, dark, even if they were a bit too loose, and made of less expensive material. His mother and father had plenty of money, John knew; he had once seen their bank statement when his father had left the Webispace connection open to his accounts. But for some reason they never seemed to kit him out with "fashist" items, or new haircuts, and not even a full selection of up-to-date thought pads to plug into the various terminals. His was a B- prototype, more than four years old, and it meant his thinking was ahead of the delivery of information through the Webispace.

He grabbed his thought pad, nonetheless, as he made his way out of the room; he would need it, he knew, for his first class.

"Whoa! Where are you off to in such a hurry, my lad?"

John had almost walked right into someone who had been standing on the other side of the door to his room. She was a cleaner, one of those dispensed by Gayle College to look after the rooms of the elite students, and—on the quiet—make sure they did not get up to too much trouble either.

"So who might you be at this early hour of the morning?"

"My name is John Broadus," John said trying to puff out his chest to assert his superiority to this mere cleaner. "I'm going to class, if it's any of your business."

"None of my business, my lad," said the cleaner. "But it might be some of your business to know that the class doesn't actually start for another half an hour. They set the alarm early on the first morning assuming that the students will ignore it at least twice before they get out of bed."

"Oh," said John, looking crestfallen and trying to think how he could recover his superiority. "I assumed I had to rush to get there on time."

"Usually," the cleaner continued, "that's a good assumption. But I see this morning we have an enthusiastic student." She said the word 'enthusiastic' as if it was a diagnosis from a medical doctor, not a description of acceptable, much less commendable, commitment.

"Sit down, lad, for a moment, while I clean your room up a bit."

John went back inside, while the cleaner began to tidy things up and clean here and there, though if truth be told there was as yet not a lot of cleaning to be done.

"Well, it's your first day," the cleaner said, "and only to be expected." She smiled encouragingly.

As she smiled John had his first opportunity to observe her. She was wearing the normal cleaner's uniform of dreary monotones, had grey hair, and when she smiled she revealed her five remaining good teeth, and one tooth darkened almost to the color of the coffee that John had just finished drinking.

"The important thing," she said as she gathered up the few items of rubbish and leftover paper, the coffee cup, and anything else that John did not hastily tell her he wanted to keep, "is to remember that things are *not* what they once were."

She glanced warily down at his thought pad, and as he touched it she immediately switched her tone.

"Well, go ahead then, Mr. Broadus, and enjoy your first class. An experience like no other." She smiled again, her voice almost happy, but it was all belied by a broad wink as she left the room just ahead of John.

"Now, then, you are an early bird, aren't you?" the professor said as he saw John sitting at the back of the room. John had arrived at his first class to find that no one else was there at all—despite the delay with the cleaner he had still arrived before anyone else, and found the room quite alone. He had wondered whether he was in the right place, until he noticed names on the desks, and right next to the terminal in which he presumed he was to plug in his thought pad was his name, unfortunately misspelt. "Broadass,"

it said. John Broadus was not sure his day could have got off to a worse start on this his first class.

"Professor," John said, "They've misspelt my name."

"Call me Dr. E.C. White," the Professor said, pointing to his name in large letters printed on the side of his expansive desk at the front of the class. "Happens all the time, don't worry about it. Look." He plugged in his, far more technical, thought pad into the terminal on his professor's desk, placed his hand on the pad, and in a blink of an eye his name shifted so that the "Wh" was replaced with a "F."

John tried to swallow back a laugh.

"That's what I found on the first day of teaching, in my first class, which was only last year, after they got rid of all the remaining teachers in the last Great Cull of illogical elements in higher education. I was young then."

John looked at him and realized that though he wore a professor's gown, he was perhaps not more than ten years older than him at most.

"Still am, I see you have noticed," Professor E.C. White said. John could see that the professor's hand was resting on the thought pad. He wondered how he had managed to read his mind.

"Anyway, yours is easy to fix." John watched as his name changed from "Broadass" to "Badass."

"Whoops," said the professor. "That's a bit better of a mistake, isn't it?" said the Professor. John was not quite sure what to say.

"Okay, there you go. Just in time." As John's name now read correctly "Broadus," the first students began arriving. They all settled into their seats, connected their thought pads, and the professor began the class.

"Now," he said out loud, "I want you to place all your hands on the thought pads. Some of your thought pads will be more advanced than others but for the purpose of this class at least, that does not matter."

Jimmy, who had sat down next to John, gave his elbow a shove at this remark, as he pointed towards John's very out-of-date, slightly tatty looking, thought pad. Jimmy then glanced at Labelle Malchance, whose thought pad was shiny bright new. Jimmy gave a comical down at mouth expression, and rubbed his right eye with his knuckle pretending little tears, as they both looked at each other's thought pads. Jimmy's was newer than John's but was still borderline archaeological.

"Connect all your thought pads and place your hands on them." Unknown to Jimmy and John, Professor White had moved from the front of the class and this last sentence was spoken right next to them in carefully enunciated, pointed, speech like a dentist drill.

"Hands connected?" said the Professor. "Good. Let's begin."

The professor placed his hand on his own thought pad, and instead of hearing his voice through their ears, immediately his voice was inside John's, and everyone else's, mind.

John was shocked. As far as he knew thought pads were for accessing the Webispace, but here something was going on about which he had prior to this no knowledge. He looked around at the others. Labelle was unfazed, Jimmy seemed a little glassy-eyed but certainly not shocked. John H. Johnson looked like he was getting ready to solve a complex algorithm for the sheer fun of it, his brow furrowed in concentration. Emily was unsmiling; Faith, though, returned his look with one of her own: eyes deliberately opened wider than normal, as if she was saying 'You ain't seen nothing yet.'

Something touched John's right foot. He looked down and Emily had reached across with her left leg to nudge him under the desk. He looked again at Emily whose face was still turned resolutely forward, and this time followed her gaze. Professor E.C. White was staring at him. John quickly returned his hand to the thought pad. Evidently not only could you hear what the professor was saying in your mind when you were connected, somehow he could tell if you were not connected and could direct his attention towards you.

"Now," the professor 'said,' though his lips did not move as he spoke, his thoughts delivered through the Webispace to the students in front of him, "On this first class for first years, my task is to introduce you to the state of New Angle Land and to begin to prepare you to combat The Contagion." There was some shifting in the seats at that remark, especially from Emily who apparently had not expected that the situation at large would so quickly be tackled head on at the very first class.

"To do that," the professor continued, perhaps not unaware of the slight stir that his remarks had caused as they were all connected jointly to the Webispace, "we will conduct a thought experiment. A thought experiment was first done by Albert Einstein, "Praise Be Upon Him," using the required respectful

'P.B.U.H' phrase, this time in full, for Einstein, whose statue was placed prominently at the front of the class, a sculpture whose image was portrayed in many public spaces in New Angle Land.

"However, unlike the scientists then, we now can go one step further thanks to the miracle," the professor stopped himself, "I mean the technology of Webispace."

"Look," the Professor said, and before the mind's eyes of the entire class was pictured not just the well-known E=MC2 equation, but a whole realm of calculations related to Einstein's General Theory of Relativity.

"Of course we now know that Einstein, PBUH, did not get everything right, but he began a process whereby we relativized knowledge, and removed any sense of absolute. This may not have been his intention, but we have gone more boldly than he meant to go. We have 'turned Einstein on his head.' Now, the thought experiment I want you to do is this. In pairs, I want you to learn not only to receive information through the Webispace but to communicate information to each other. To make it harder one of you will have a negative message, for instance making the last name of your fellow student into something absurd," at this Professor White smiled at John Broadus, "while the other student will attempt to counteract that with positive thoughts, about his own name, so that his last name retains its basic integrity and spelling. You will see soon enough that positive thoughts are a most important weapon against The Contagion."

A mental image of a hand being raised came from the direction of Emily. Emily did not raise her actual physical hand, that was still attached to the thought pad, but somehow she managed to project through the Webispace the image of her hand so that the professor could see it, and so could the other students.

"Impressive, Ms. Lee. You are learning quickly." Emily smiled. "Perhaps too quickly. What is it that you want?"

"I would like to know, sir, what is this 'Contagion' that you are talking about, at least in your own view."

There was a mental pause for a heartbeat. Then the professor thought back through the Webispace. "The Contagion, Ms. Lee, is whatever the Cognitive Police determine to be negative and thought crimes against the New Angle Land way."

"And what's the New Angle Land way?" asked John Broadus. Another hushed mental silence, this time not as a surprise of approval but some Webispace mutual surprise of disbelief. One or two heads even turned in his direction, though all the students still kept their hands resting on the thought pads, and once the professor began to speak quickly looked towards the front of the class again.

"You must be a first year Mr. Broadass." He said the last syllable of his name with enough distinction that John noticed the way he was spelling it, and one or two others did as well. "The New Angle Land way is the way of peace wrought by the removal of all public expressions of religion."

"If this has given us so much peace, why is there now a Contagion?" said Faith Felicity, 'speaking' for the first time.

"Because, Ms. Fait Felicity," the Professor removed the 'h' from what he said and shortened the vowel sound to make it close enough to 'fat' to cause Faith to blush as he spoke. "Because not everyone is able to stay positive. Some doubt. Some cannot stop doubting. The infection spreads."

"Is that what they call Episteme?" said 'H', the letter H. on his name John H. Johnson underlined cleverly as he spoke into the Webispace.

"Yes, Mr. Johnson, it is. Serial doubters eventually catch the Episteme mind virus. They may even become Epistemic. But now for more positive things. We will leave that up to the Cognitive Police. Your task as I have explained is to grow in your positive thinking powers by doing mental battle, within confined and safe environments, one to one in your class room situation now. Choose your partner and begin your mental joust. The winners will compete against each other, until we have the two best doing mental positive battle, and the winner of that will get this." He pointed down at a brand new thought pad beside him.

"That's an A+!" said Jimmy.

"Yes, it is. And now, begin."

One by one the students paired off and began to try to out positively think their partners, the winner being indicated by a ridiculous, humorous, or negative, reworking of the letters of the names of the person with whom they were battling. Soon enough John had turned Jimmy's last name into "Cowman."

Whether by happenstance, beginner's luck, or some innate as yet undiscovered ability, John Broadus continued to work his way up the list of fellow students. Someone whose last name was "Grance" was renamed to "Trance"; another student whose last name was "Timise" was renamed to "Timid."

Finally, it was just John Broadus and "H." (John H. Johnson). "H" had advanced to the last stage so quickly because he had insisted on using his name simply as "H", an abbreviated single letter which made turning it to something ludicrous particularly difficult. As John and H. mentally faced each other, images in their minds now forming of two knights about to do battle, replaced by sumo wrestlers at H's mental suggestion, and then by cowboys about to draw guns at high noon at the mental suggestion of John, the professor inserted a pause into the mental fight.

"Now," he said, "we will see who will win the A+ thought pad, to open you to a higher level of mental reasoning. Remember against the Contagion, staying positive is everything. I want no epistemic individuals among my class. You are the elite, to fight the Contagion. Well, then, once more: begin."

As he said 'begin,' he removed the mental pause to once again allow them to joust mentally, and their images of two battling individuals circled and replaced one another in the minds of all the students watching—knights on their horses readying to joust, quickly replaced by two sumo wrestlers circling about each other ready to grapple, then two cowboys with their gun belts hung low ready to draw and fire their six shooters.

The mental battle began. H. was clearly the mentally superior, and he had the better more advanced thought pad too which allowed him to make suggestions and counter negativity at a far faster rate than John Broadus. John however, would not give up, and with each suggestion and counter-suggestion—several times he thought 'ache' to add to 'h', or 'hat', mentally picturing a silly feather hat on top of H.—John resolutely seemed to inch closer to mentally sidestepping his opponent.

The other students sat watching fascinated by the circling pictures of combatants, and the mental verbal jousting accompanying them. H. attempted "Broadass" again, but this time John was ready, and countered with "hippy," adding "ippy" in front of H.'s name. Everyone started laughing, H. included. John Broadus had won.

"Well done, John," the professor said. "You not only have a mental speed of thought, and determination, you have a sense of humour too. All of those ingredients will help as you—all of you," he said mentally scanning around the class as he concluded, "fight the Contagion. When the class is over you can gather your new thought pad."

"An A+" said Jimmy.

"Yes, Mr. *Cowman*, A+. Now it is time to return to work. And I will project to you the reading you are to do for the remainder of the class. *Lessons in Logical Positivity*, by E.N. Darrow. You will find her insights fascinating."

The rest of the class passed without much interest for John Broadus, or, it appeared, for many of the other students, as they scanned down the data download, and made mental notes through the nodes of their thought pad for later scanning and further assimilation. The professor had called the reading fascinating, but as far as John could see it was deadly dull. And not particularly logical, either.

However, it was not until the end of the class—when everyone had momentarily managed to disconnect from their thought pads—that John gained further insight into what had taken place during his first class at Gayle. Nor until then did he begin to suspect that the cleaner, with her suggestion that things at Gayle were not as they once were, might be on to something.

John went up to the front desk to collect his A+. The professor looked at him cautiously.

"I'll be keeping this Mr. Broadus," he said.

"What do you mean," said John, "I thought that was the prize for winning."

"Yes, so it is, but I am not sure that you deserve it. I thought I detected some unmeliorated negativity behind the mental jousting, not just a game, but something unrefined. I will be watching you carefully Mr. Broadus. If you prove yourself worthy, then I will pass you this A+ thought pad. Until then," he looked down at the tatty unit that John was clutching in his right hand, "I think you have all that you require at your stage of development."

He turned around and left through the professors' exit at the back of the classroom.

"What do you mean he didn't give it to you?" said Jimmy as they walked out together, with Emily alongside.

"Apparently, I have further development before I am worthy."

"But it was a prize that you won fair and square," said Emily, "He can't keep it back from you. He promised!"

"He also said he would be watching me carefully. Apparently, I have unmitigated or something elements of negativity behind the mental jousting."

"*Unmeliorated,*" Emily and Jimmy said together.

"That's bad," said Emily.

"Uh-huh," said Jimmy.

"What do you mean?" said John.

"What *he* means is," said Emily, "he thinks you might be open to a Contagion." She looked around as the students bustled pass her on their way to break before the next class began. "Come in here."

They slipped into an alcove just out of sight—and earshot—of the students crushing together as they bustled their way down the corridors.

"Make sure you don't touch the wall. They are meant to indicate when something is a vehicle to connect to the Webispace, like a public thought pad, but you can never be sure. I've heard someone say that much of the physical space of public buildings is now wired into the Webispace."

"What about the floor, then?" said John. Emily looked down at his shoes.

"As long as your shoes are the old-fashioned non-webified standard shoes you should be fine. If you are barefoot, you can never tell; and if you have those new wired shoes…"

"Or clothes," said Jimmy.

"Yep," said Emily. "Listen did you notice something today in the class?"

"Like what?" said John.

"I mean something missing. Something you would expect to find in most classrooms."

"Certainly in the good old days," added Jimmy. "The sort of thing you might have heard about growing up, and expected to counter a lot of in a classroom at an elite college like Gayle."

John thought for a little bit. "Books," he said, "there were no books."

"There's no library either," said Emily. "I've checked. Or if there is I haven't managed to find it yet."

Jimmy and John looked at her quizzically.

"I got here a day early and I've been looking around," she explained.

"No books," said John, "and no library."

"At least not one we've managed to locate yet," Emily carried on. "Everything now is webified. You just connect to a portal, anywhere and there you are."

"That sounds great," said John. "I mean, talk about easy access. No more lugging your books around."

"It *was* great" said Jimmy.

"But now it's changed. The Webispace does not just download information to you. It records the information you download to it. In other words," Emily trailed off looking over her shoulder to make sure she was not being overheard.

"In other words," John finished for her, "it can read your thoughts."

Chapter Four

THE COUNCIL

When The Council met it was only ever in secret. The apparatus of democracy was still fully in place across New Angle Land— there were votes, and elections, and candidates, and parties with different policies about which the less informed spent considerable time arguing. Every four years, as was traditional now, a new candidate would be chosen as Leader of New Angle Land, a regular replacement strategy long since agreed upon by The Council, which seemed to underline the voice of the people in the government. In reality, the leadership of New Angle Land had not changed for decades, and all the truly important decisions were taken at meetings like this one, secretive, in the belly of the underground Crypt, converted from its previous use, to house the secretive meetings of The Council.

Inevitably, such a location gave its meetings an eerie feeling, but its great advantage was that no one had yet thought to wire the crypt beneath the old Cathedral into the wider Webispace, so that conversations here were not intruded upon by the techniques of mental surveillance and counter surveillance that was now normal throughout the rest of New Angle Land. They sat in the middle, around a round table, knights of the realm, an earlier council member had joked, to not much laughter, for in reality like the rest of New Angle Land there was little democracy here either. The chair called the meeting, led the meeting, ratified any decisions of the meeting, had the last word, and the casting vote. There was no vice chair, no secretary, no parliamentary procedure, no minutes, and the rest of the Council was there to execute the will of the whole council together which was, except in extraordinary circumstances, the will of the chair truly.

Up above them music, muffled, could still be heard. Another advantage of this meeting place, late at night, was that the noise in the Cathedral, converted now as all the old cathedrals had been to an Amusement Zone, would silence any noise from beneath, and make overhearing the deliberations of the Council, if they did truly deliberate, next to impossible.

Each Council member was identified as he arrived by a DNA scan, an individualized means of ensuring that no subterfuge took place as the Council members did not show each other their faces. Long since it had been set up as protocol that the 12 members of the Council were empowered to select their own replacements, and from early days The Council had included select members of the judiciary, the army, the government, and the police. But when they met, to prevent any chance of them being mutually discovered if one were compromised, their faces were covered, and their voices muffled beneath an electronic cloaking device inserted into their identical hoods. For, yes, they did speak: all thought pads were left at the entrance to the crypt, ensuring that this meeting—alone of important meetings in New Angle Land—was immune from the eavesdropping of the Walkers, and other techniques of snooping, which had, of course, been themselves set in motion by the Council. They spoke, and they listened; they did not transmit their thoughts (in this room) via the Webispace. That, they knew, was *their* means of finding out was going on, and they did not want their own guns unknowingly turned upon themselves by any underground subversive movement—if any such thing could happen.

Their clothes were white, surpluses that went down to their ankles, covering all the external trappings of fashion and body shape; their hoods were also white, with a single emblem on the forehead above their eyes, interlocking spirals of a double helix, indicating the DNA that they each had offered before they entered the Council chamber in the Crypt. As they went into the room, each Council member offered his bare arm to an elderly attendant, his face not in shadow, nor covered, but revealed, though he never, it was ensured, saw the Council members' faces, but whose service had been so long that none questioned his presence at this point. He shuffled forward towards each Council member, took a blood sample, fed the blood into a hand held device that read out the match to the Council members' DNA. Their secrecy was maintained by a simple ruse: their real DNA was not on record, only here, and only matched by the words "Council Member" that appeared as each blood offering was paid, was their DNA recorded in reality.

Last of all came in The Chair. It was his prerogative to arrive last, by long tradition, and his place was reserved around the round table, with no chair at its location, for the Chair came in on a wheelchair. Whether he had always been unable to walk, or had suffered an accident in the Wars of Religion that had preceded the rule of New Angle Land and its way, was unknown to the rest of the Council, as, of course, was his identity. He came in last; he left last. There was an honorific five minute pause after the meeting had ended before he would leave the Council chamber; there was always an exact five minute pause before he entered after the last Council member had arrived. In this straightforward way his precedence and status was maintained, as he wheeled in, manually, no thought pad involved, no computer either in this the Council Chamber, he was last to leave, last to arrive, and when he spoke the others listened.

Thudding music from above in the Cathedral Amusement Zone provided a background muffle as the Council, now all arrived, awaited in silence for the arrival of the Chair. Five minutes precisely passed, and he wheeled (they assumed it was he) himself into the Council Chamber, and around the table to his place. Everyone sat down in their seats as he touched his hands to the table, and when the scraping of chairs had ceased, and all the heads in all the white robes turned towards the Chair, there was once again silence (bar the Amusement Zone frolics from above).

"Despite our best efforts," the Chair began, his voice altered by the device in his hood so that it appeared flat and dull, lifeless, and of indeterminate gender, as well as character. Nonetheless, he (if it was he) had a way of speaking which ensured attention, if only because those who did not give it attention were rarely allowed any prominence in the Council, and sometimes their terms were cut short, an indication only knowable to each other if the replacement person was of a remarkably different stature to his or her predecessor. "Despite our best efforts, the mental infection known as the Contagion is spreading. Each day we hear new reports of individuals developing doubt, lack of purpose, meaning, and commitment to the New Angle Land way. Such persons appear rapidly to lose all drive for work or study, become listless, uneconomically productive, and develop what we have called 'epistemic' characteristics. We have attempted quarantine, isolating such individuals within communities where the infection is already rife and so no further damage can be done—for it appears that this intellectual tendency, like a virus, is able to spread from person to person. When such quarantine is ineffective, as it has proved with new outbreaks of epistemic individuals each day, we have begun a process of removing individuals from social interaction in the wider society altogether, putting them into our cognitive crime prisons, even in solitary confinement.

"This epistemic infection shows no sign of abating. We have limited, if not entirely removed, all access to information—books" (at this word, even his electronically altered voice managed a sneer), "and the like, long since channeling our society's choices to the limitless expanse of the Webispace, with countless aspects of information and viewing constantly available, none of which suggests any possibility of divergence from the New Angle Land way. Despite all this, all our best efforts I say, the Contagion has begun, and has spread, and is not abating. It is time for a new, and more radical, strategy. It is time for this."

An image appeared in the middle of the Council, twirling in the central area of the round table, an image which immediately drew gasps of electronically modified horror from the Council. "Don't worry," The Chair said, "this is not connected to the Webispace."

"How can we be sure?" a voice from across the Chamber asked. Who spoke was indicated by a number before him on the table, each Council member having a number from 1-12 at their place, with the Chair indicated by, of course, number 1. The question came from 9.

"Sure?" The Chair said, turning his chair slightly to look across at 9. The silence froze around the room, as if the actual temperature in the room dropped at his speaking, the cool Crypt atmosphere moved from the fridge to the freezer. "You are sure because I say you are sure."

Attention turned back to the image twirling in the middle of the Council. It was clearly an epistemic individual, or at least how the Council viewed an epistemic person. He appeared deranged, rabid almost, angry, and yet at the same time devoid of purpose. He was shown doing nothing at his desk at work, and angrily shouting at the Cognitive Police when they came to test his cognitive positivity through their thought pad test, and then railed and fought as he was led away by the Cognitive Police to a Cognitive Crime Prison.

Next, the image changed. Apparently, it was the same person, yet this time he looked calm. He was clothed in neat, white, clothes; unfashionable, but clean and tidy. He was sitting at a desk, a "responder" in a call center for the "Webispace," speaking through the Webispace, connected appropriately by a portal connected to his updated thought pad, and giving instructions to those having difficulties with this or that feature of the Webispace. And the instructions, far from being epistemic, listless, purposeless, much less angry or disillusioned, were now constantly positive, calm. The epistemic individual was no longer epistemic. He had been placed back in society as a functional member of the hive.

"Can it be done?" said number 6.

"Yes," said The Chair, "It can be done. *If we will it.*" The Chair began to explain the technique, and what it would take to achieve such a change on an individual level, and then on a mass scale. As he talked on and on into the night, with the music pounding above from the Amusement Zone in the Cathedral, the air in Crypt of the Council chamber appeared to drop, if it was possible, even a degree or two cooler. The Council members, some of them, began to visibly shiver a little, turning their heads to one another as the Chair described what would have to take place to turn an epistemic individual to such a useful member of society as they had witnessed in the image in front of them. Around the room the entombed bodies of ancient aristocracy, and bishops, and once famous or wealthy patrons of the Cathedral, as it used to be, lay still, holding their breath if they had had breath to hold, lying still if they had any choice to do other. The shadows behind the Chair shifted, a little, as if there were a ghost hiding its shaped apparition, and covering its phantasmal ears, so that it too might not have to consider such an option as was being outlined with confidence and conviction by the Chair from his wheelchair, number 1, to each of the other numbers of the Council, hooded in their white surpluses, covered from head to foot, prevented from showing any sense of shame, or blushing, or raising an eyebrow, or looking shocked.

After the Chair had finished speaking, he looked around the room, and called for a decision. Hands were raised in favor, but not many, his, of course, number 6, and number 2, and number 9– cowed into obedience by his previous confrontation with the Chair. The others raised their hands to say no to this new, more radical, strategy. Once the decision had been taken they began to leave the room in strict order, starting with number 12, until the Chair was alone in the room. Before 2 had left he had turned to face the Chair and a barely perceptible nod from the Chair answered his inquiry. Once he had exited the Council chamber as well the Chair remained where he was. This time, for the first time in living memory, he waited six minutes before leaving too. He carried with him a piece of paper, with each of the numbers of the Council on it, and little cross marks next to each of the numbers who had opposed his proposal. With quick strokes of his pen he struck a line through each of those opposition numbers. Himself, 2, 6, and 9 were left. "The rest," The Chair allowed himself to say out loud once the traditional five minutes had passed, "can be replaced."

John woke with a start. He was drenched in sweat, and as he awoke his heart had given an enormous thud which had echoed throughout this chest cavity like a canon. He had been dreaming, at least that is what he thought it was, but the dream had seemed so real that he felt he had been almost present in the eerie, underground, cavern, where men in white robes spoke in electronically muffled tones about a 'more radical solution' to the Contagion.

He went down to breakfast, feeling about as rested as a piece of laundry does after it has been put through a wash cycle. He was all tumbled and turned, inside and out, and when he sat down next to Emily and Jimmy they looked across at him questioningly.

"What happened to you?" said Jimmy, "you look about as happy as I feel after I've eaten my mum's cooking."

"That's a horrible thing to say about your mum!" said Emily. "What's wrong with your mum's cooking anyway?"

"Look at him and you'll get the idea," said Jimmy, "it makes you feel like that. Apart from apple pie. She does a mean apple pie," he added, and a dreamy faraway expression came over Jimmy's face. "Rest of the time, though," he said coming back down to earth, "she makes you look like that." He pointed at John.

"I'm fine," said John.

"You are obviously *not* fine!" said Emily, "Something's bitten you…You look, well…you look like you've seen a ghost."

"I saw something. When I was asleep." John explained the glimpses of shadowy figures in eerie white robes in a creepy underground cavern, and their 'more radical solution' to the Contagion.

"It's just a dream, mate," said Jimmy. "When I eat my mum's soup I usually have nightmares. What?" he said looking at Emily who was giving him a most disapproving stare. "I do!"

"Anyway," said Emily, "Jimmy is probably right. It probably was just a dream, though it does sound like a particularly nasty one."

"It wasn't a dream. It was real. If anything this feels more like a dream than that."

"Thanks a lot John! Are we figments of your imagination, then?"

"No I don't mean that…I just mean, well, it wasn't a dream. Can the Webispace take your thoughts and connect you to other places?"

Emily looked across at John with concern in her eyes. "I don't think so John, at least I've never heard of it."

"You know what you need? You need something to take your mind off it." Jimmy thought for a moment. "I have an idea."

It was Saturday so there were no classes that morning at Gayle College, and Jimmy led them down to the back entrance to the main campus of Gayle College, and down a side street, and there parked behind a house was a car. Not any old car, though.

Jimmy opened it up with a touch of his hand against the side thought panel.

"This is *yours*?" said John.

"Yep." Jimmy looked at it lovingly.

"How on earth can you afford it?" Emily asked.

"Because," Jimmy said, "it's my dad's."

"I thought you said it was yours?"

"What I mean," said Jimmy, "is that it's mine for the weekend! Come on get in."

It was the fastest looking thing that John had ever seen. His parents' car was just a car, a box to get your from A to B with minimum fuss and hassle. It was not bought for speed, or for looks, much less to impress other people when it went by. This car, though, was different. At Jimmy's loving touch on the main thought pad console at the front of the car it rose briskly, hovering above the ground in its start position, hardly making a sound, apart from a satisfyingly reassuring click and whirr of the engine barely turning over.

"Get a load of this!" said Jimmy. And they took off into the morning air, shooting from one level of the New Angle Land airway to another, shortcutting through the thought lanes that appeared inside the minds of the drivers and passengers as they were connected to the cars, and did not block the view of the inhabitants of New Angle Land far below. As yet there were few other cars in the airway and so they had the road to themselves. They began to pick up speed.

"Now," said Jimmy, "the important thing to remember about driving these Taurus Titans is that what counts is acceleration not sheer speed. Speed can get you into trouble," he nodded at a maximum speed sign that whisked past them as they kept on roaring along. "But," he continued, "if you slow down, come off the airway to a subsidiary road," he did precisely that as he talked, "and then back onto the airway at the next exit, and then," he said loudly, "you can hit it!" An expression of concentration came over Jimmy's face and the car roared into action, and Emily and John were slammed against their seats in the back, barely missing falling embarrassingly into each other's arms.

"Sorry," said John, extricating himself from Emily.

"Sorry! You're sorry! What about dufus ball over there," she pointed at Jimmy, "don't you think he should be sorry! Scared the living daylights out of me!"

"That's the idea," said Jimmy, the car now cruising along at just below speed limit level. "Of course even acceleration can get you into trouble so you have to be careful," he said scanning around for the police. "Anyway, who else wants a go?" he turned around to look at John and Emily in the back seat.

"No way!" said Emily, "take us back to Gayle College right away…and I mean do it without killing us!"

"I'll have a go," said John.

"John!" said Emily

"That's the idea, John," Jimmy pulled over to the side and they swapped seats. "Now remember to enjoy yourself. Take your mind off things. Let go. Feel the breeze through your hair."

"Breeze!" said Emily, "when you did it, it was more like a blooming hurricane!"

John settled himself into the seat, put his hand on the thought pad, and the car began to take off into the airways once again, travelling up through the different zones, and negotiating the traffic with sensibility and dignity.

"That's more like it, that's what I call a nice Saturday morning drive." Emily settled into her seat and put her arms above her head. "Easy does it. Easy like Saturday morning."

"Yuck," said Jimmy. "Come on John, stop being such a wimp, punch that thought pad and let's get going." John peered around at Jimmy, and slowly took the car off an exit lane, onto a side road, and maneuvered around to get back onto the main airway again.

"John," said Emily, "Don't pay attention to Jimmy. Take it easy. Easy. EASY!"

The last word was spoken more as a scream, as John 'punched' the thought pad, in his mind, and the Taurus Titan accelerated with such velocity that even Jimmy was caught by surprise.

"That's it John, let it all out, blow off some steam." They continued to accelerate dramatically, "Of course" he added, "I don't actually want to *die*... at least not today." Emily was silently shaking now. "Okay, John," said Jimmy, "I think that's enough." The car kept accelerating.

"John" he shouted, "slow down."

"John? JOHN!" Jimmy reached forward and grabbed John's hands from off the thought pad, put his own hand on it instead, and steered the car back off the airway into a side street, and parked the car on the ground. A police car drove past them, hesitated for a moment, and then kept on going.

"Phew," said Jimmy, "that was a close thing. My dad would have killed me if I'd got a ticket."

"Killed you?" said Emily, "KILLED you? In a moment he wouldn't have had to have bothered. You'd have been dead already!" She looked over towards John, annoyed in the extreme.

"She's got a point you know," said Jimmy. There was no reply. "John? John?"

A couple of hours later John woke up in his room, lying on his bed, and saw his two friends Jimmy and Emily looking down at him with concern.

"He's coming around," said Emily.

"Just keep him away from my dad's car," said Jimmy.

John mumbled something. Jimmy leaned closer. "What was that? What did he say? Was it sorry I almost killed you both, wrecked your car, and what's worse got you into trouble with your dad?"

"I had a dream," said John.

"I had a nightmare," said Jimmy.

"I mean," said John, "I was there again."

"Where?" said Emily.

"In the Council, in the chamber, in that eerie dark place. He's going to do it anyway."

"Do what?" said Emily, looking with wide open eyes at John, while Jimmy came a little closer so he could hear better.

"He's going to take the 'more radical solution' anyway. He marked each of the Council members who disagreed with him. He crossed their names out off the list. He said, 'they can be replaced.' I think he's going to kill them so he can deal with the Contagion more radically anyway, with or without their support. He's going to replace them."

"No idea what you mean," said Jimmy still looking a little angry at the danger he had found himself in only a few moments ago.

"Come on," said Emily, "All's well that ends well. Let's go down to the Common Room and see what's happening with everyone else." The Common Room was one of the most connected spaces at Gayle College, with every thought pad terminal functioning at highest speed (though none were A+), and multiple game zones so that students could play against each other.

That evening, the Webispace was hosting a live New Angle Land wide episode of mind frisbi, where students competed against each other across New Angle Land. There were other zones for games too: none of them particularly appealed to Emily, Jimmy, or John, not even though mind frisbi was accompanied by loud renditions of cheers and back slaps as Gayle College combatants marched forwards to the penultimate round that evening.

For a while Jimmy and John played mind chess, while Emily watched, a game where not only were pieces moved mentally across the board, but part of the challenge was hiding your own thoughts, reading your competitor's thoughts, so that experts not only thought several moves ahead, but could effectively predict what the other player was thinking several moves in advance, and then change their plan in concordance, and vice versa up through several interchanges of difficulty. The national level players worked at a ten level interchange, as each thought ahead, predicted each other's moves, changed their plan, and so on, ten times over. Jimmy and John were only working on a level two, and that, after their experience in the Taurus Titan was quite exhausting enough. After a little while, they gave up and moved to a corner of the Common Room where the noise levels were lower, and there were fewer other students around.

Jimmy sat down next to John, slapped him on the back, and said, "Well, it was a little…well, more than a little…scary, but no hard feelings me old mate." They shook hands. Emily sat down opposite them.

"Look," she said. On the table between them was the usual round up of current events—events that the Webispace thought would be of interest, at least—and right at the top of the list of recurring items at that moment was this headline:

"MORE RADICAL SOLUTION NEEDED, SAYS POLICE CHIEF"

The phrase 'more radical solution' was familiar to them all after John's recount of his dream. They looked at each other. Emily expanded the article underneath the headline by touching the thought pad and thinking it open. Underneath the story continued.

"The head of Police of New Angle Land has announced that in his view there is a need for more radical solutions to the Contagion.

'We must stop this before it gets any worse', he said, 'we cannot afford to mess around anymore. It's time for something more radical before it is too late and it all gets out of hand.'"

At this point Emily stopped reading it aloud to John and Jimmy.

"Look," she said. They followed where she was pointing with her other hand as she maximized the last sentence of the piece so they could see it easily.

"The chief of police was speaking," the sentence read, *"after his appointment following the sudden unexpected demise of his predecessor who died yesterday."*

"But how can that be possible?" said Emily. "He was a young man. It doesn't even say how he died, or what killed him. How can his successor have been appointed so quickly?"

"Because," said John, "It wasn't a dream. The Chair is beginning to replace the Council members who didn't agree with him."

"Maybe," Jimmy murmured unconvinced.

"Either way," said Emily, "someone wants a more radical solution. That doesn't sound good."

Chapter Five

DISAPPEARANCES AT GAYLE COLLEGE

Because Saturday had been so stressful for John, Sunday was mostly spent in bed, apart from the compulsory Sunday morning exercises. There was no chapel at Gayle College anymore—rumour had it that in the old days there used to be such things—but instead there was Citizenship and Patriotism Lesson (otherwise known as CAPL), where you were taught the ideals of New Angle Land. They all paraded into the Great Hall once more, their shoddy late Sunday morning sleepiness hidden beneath their Gayle College dark gowns, and listened as the president effusively described the virtues expected. "Positivity," he said, "*always* be positive."

"*Positively* boring more like," said Jimmy, as he and John walked out with the rest of the students after they had finished singing the Gayle College song. John grunted in agreement as he made his way back up to his room to catch up with his sleep.

Later that afternoon, after John had woken up sufficiently to string together a sentence or two, Emily and John and Jimmy met together. In between the buildings of the main campus area of Gayle College there was a large, grassy expanse, called the quad. That afternoon first years had gathered for a pick up game of mind frisbi, unlike the computerized version in the common room this entailed mental control of a physical object through the Webispace. Gerald Hawthorne, a massive burly third year, had been delegated to instruct first years in the difficult art. Labelle Malchance jogged up to join the crowd gathering to learn how to play mind frisbi, along with Faith Felicity; John H. Johnson watched warily from the side.

"Now," said Gerald, "this is not at all like that pretend game that you saw yesterday in the common room. Anyone can do that. *This*," he said taking out a shimmering, translucent disc, "is a mind frisbi. It is aerially linked to the Webispace so that every time you touch it you reconnect and have a 10 second control established. For those ten seconds you can send the frisbi wherever you want." As he said this, the mind frisbi left his hand and went up, hovered, and passed quickly behind John H. Johnson's head and started to flap from side to side. "However," Gerald continued, "once the ten seconds are up your connection is severed." The disc flopped to the ground behind H. with a clang so that he turned around, noticed it for the first time, and looked back comically at the others in surprise. "What's more," said Gerald, "as my friend here will demonstrate," he indicated a smaller third year whose name was Barry Dunlop, "there is an added complication." Barry picked up the mind frisbi, established connection, flew it to Gerald who also linked up. "For the time that our two connections overlap," Gerald spoke as the mind frisbi hovered between Barry and Gerald, "one of the two controllers either has to relinquish control of the frisbi or, if they are not on the same team, battle for ownership." At this a concentrated look appeared on the faces of Barry and Gerald and the frisbi began to vibrate and its colors shifted to represent the characteristics of Barry and Gerald in turn, first one then the other, with their faces appearing on the top of the disc, and then disappearing, until after a mental battle Gerald's burly form was dominant and the disc flew steadily back to his outstretched reach.

"Other than that," said Gerald, "it's just like the game you played, some of you, in the common room last night. It's five a side, there is a goal at either end, and the team that outscores the opposition over the hour wins. You cannot run holding the frisbi," he said smiling patronizingly at Faith Felicity who was running backwards and forwards with enthusiasm waiting to begin. "But you have to move into position so that you can receive the frisbi passed by your team member. Of course there is another way to break into the control of your opponent." Gerald moved over to Barry who was balancing the frisbi an inch or two from his outstretched hand in a display calculated to impress Labelle Malchance who was looking at him with wide eyed admiration. While Barry was facing the other way he gave him a big shove in the back, and the frisbi fell with a clatter to the ground. "You can 'distract' him," he said. "Right, break up into teams of five and I will be watching to see who has what it takes and who," he looked across at H. "almost certainly doesn't."

The games began with frenetic enthusiasm, though unfortunately to start with most of the first years could not even get the frisbi to move more than a yard or two away from their grasp before it flopped unceremonially to the ground. There was not exactly much in the way of action to begin with, and Gerald Hawthorne paced the sidelines of the frisbi court marked out in the middle of the large Gayle College quad with something like exasperation, or frustration, on his big, broad, face. Several sets of five teams had had their brief chance to show what they could do, and then John Broadus joined, along with Emily and Jimmy.

"Come on H.," he said looking across at John H. Johnson standing some distance from the action, "join in." H. shook his head and looked away. "Alright, well let's make the most of this."

"Here goes nothing," said Jimmy.

"Let's at least *try*," said Emily.

Emily was given the mind frisbi to start the game, and after some attempts she just managed to make the frisbi flop over to Jimmy without it hitting the ground.

"Not bad," shouted Gerald, looking Emily up and down, "Not bad at all." John felt a feeling like burning in his stomach.

"Here," said Jimmy, and somehow he managed to make the frisbi shudder slowly across to John. "Not exactly like watching the National New Angle Land team play, is it? Still, I suppose we all have to start somewhere. Don't worry, John, if you can't do anything with it this time," he added as John caught the frisbi in his outstretched hand, "after all you are a *firster*," he said loudly enough for the rest of the team and Gerald Hawthorne to hear, "no one can expect much of you this time." Jimmy glanced across at Labelle Malchance, whose perfectly manicured hair was sparkling in the light and who appeared to have just walked out of a fashion shoot.

John stared down at the frisbi in his hand, and thought for a moment. Suddenly he felt connected. The mind frisbi hovered immediately inches from his hand, he saw an opening ten yards ahead, next to Faith on the opposite team, and spun the frisbi mentally in that direction. As it soared John's face was perfectly etched on to its surface indicating his appropriate complete control of the disc. Faith attempted to intercept the frisbi by jumping for it to prevent it going into the unmarked goal, but as she jumped, with just two seconds left on John's mind control time allotment, John managed to mentally move the frisbi again, away from her reach, and pummeled it through the goal.

There was a pause as everyone stared at John. And then applause!

"Wow, mate," said Jimmy, "I take it all back. Next time I will expect a lot more of you."

Gerald Hawthorne raced up and slapped John on the back. "You," he said with emphasis, "have potential."

That evening in the common room, quiet now as everyone was meant to be preparing for the class the next morning, Emily and Jimmy sat next to John in silence as they looked over the Webispace schedule, and studied for their first lesson in NALL (New Angle Land Logic). *Lessons in Logical Positivity*, by E.N. Darrow was the textbook, though, of course, there was no "book", merely a Webispace interactive text downloaded through their thought pads to their minds. Emily and Jimmy sat with John as each scanned through the information that scrolled down their minds, and mentally took notes for recording their conclusions for discussion tomorrow. Darrow was mentally saying to Emily, "The difference between logical positivity, and logical negativity is simple and essential: any resulting conclusion that puts down an individual cannot truly be deemed logical by the principles of logical positivity." Emily stifled a yawn. She nudged John, whose eyes were similarly glazed over as he tried to keep up with E.N. Darrow's exposition of logical positivity, and who in turn nudged Jimmy, whose eyes were—if it were possible—actually shut while the mental scroll of Darrow's voice was projected to his mind.

"*Oi!*" said Emily, "You can't expect to learn anything while you're asleep!"

"I wasn't asleep," said Jimmy, a little defensively, rubbing his eyes, "My eyes were shut in concentration. The truly mentally gifted," he continued, "can do both, you know."

"Perhaps they can," said Emily, "but you're not H.!"

They all glanced across to H. who was at the same time scanning through Darrow, taking mental notes, practicing his piano lessons, and previewing the next week's set of classes in *Art for Art's Sake* by Ursula R. Kiddn.

Emily disengaged from the thought pad, and John and Jimmy followed suit, disconnecting as well. "Let's go for a walk to clear our minds," Emily said.

Outside of the Common Room Emily led the way back to the alcove where they had stood on the first day after their first class. Once more they were careful not to touch the walls, in case they might unknowingly engage with the Webispace.

"I still haven't found a library, even the remains of an old one," she said.

"We didn't know you were still looking," said Jimmy. "Did we John—When do you manage to fit all this in anyway? We've been working hard, what with frisbi," he raised an eyebrow at John with this remark, "fast cars, and of course," he hastily added "studying *very* hard too."

"Unlike some of you I get up early," Emily crossed her arms. "Anyway, so far no library. I just thought I should let you know."

"I wonder what a book would be like," said John.

"Don't go wondering out loud away from here," Jimmy said quickly, "They'll think you are definitely trouble. Dr. White will have you marked down as epistemic positive before you can blink."

"Oh come on," said Emily, "He's not that bad!"

"Who? Dr. White or John? *E.C. Fite*," John had told them about the misspelling of the Professor's name, "by name, gets into a fight easily by nature."

"Anyway," said John, "I won't talk about it anywhere else. But I do wonder, that's all."

"So do I," said Emily.

"So do we all," said Jimmy insincerely, "perhaps it would be easier to doze off to without some guy droning on in your mind while you're trying to catch up on your sleep." Jimmy started to make his way out of the alcove.

"Before we disband this little meeting," Emily smiled, touching Jimmy lightly on the arm, "I have one other thing to say. Have you noticed," she began, "where is Barry Dunlop?"

"You mean the third year who couldn't catch a turnip with a pitchfork?" said Jimmy.

"*Yes*," said Emily, "I mean the one who was helping us learn frisbi this afternoon."

"What do you mean where is he, it's only been a few hours since we last saw him," John asked.

"His room is next to John H. Johnson's room and H. told me he didn't come in to change after the frisbi this afternoon."

"And he wasn't at dinner," said Jimmy

"And he wasn't in the common room," said John.

"Strange, that's all I'm saying," Emily added at last, as they walked out of the alcove back to the common room to prepare for their NALL class the next morning.

When morning arrived, Emily, John, and Jimmy sat down together in their usual places for breakfast in the Great Hall.

"Getting into a rut are we?" said Jimmy as he started to munch through his cereal, and sip loudly at his coffee.

"Could you eat a little more *quietly*, you know less like a railway engine going into a railway car," Emily made a disgusted face as

Jimmy continued to slurp his way through breakfast. Jimmy started to make 'toot-toot' noises at each mouthful as well, just to annoy Emily. She turned away from him and looked towards John.

John was staring down at his plate where, instead of food, was a brown parcel. "How did that get here?" he asked out loud.

"What is it?" said Emily.

"I have no idea," said John, "It's just here. I noticed it when I sat down. In my usual place."

"Do you think it's meant for you?" said Jimmy, though it sounded more like 'dyoushinkitshmenforu' as he continued to eat without a break while he spoke.

"Perhaps next breakfast I should bring an umbrella," said Emily pretending to brush off food residue from the arm next to Jimmy. "I don't think you should open it. How do you know it's for you?"

"Because on the outside it says 'John Broadus,' " said John.

"Ah," said Jimmy, his interest now sufficiently aroused that he had stopped eating for a moment. "*Maybe* it is meant for him," sarcastically winking at Emily.

"At least don't open it here," said Emily glancing around. "I still haven't heard that they've found Barry. In fact," she added nervously, "no one seems to have noticed that's he not here anymore, apart from us and H. It's like no one cares."

"Or wants to look like they care" said Jimmy.

"Exactly," said Emily, "So *don't* open it here, John. There's something funny going on."

By now Faith Felicity, and Labelle Malchance, and one or two other students had observed their whispered, excited, interaction, and were staring over towards them. John pretended to carry on eating, leaning over his plate lazily and sleepily, and with his arm half hiding the brown parcel, with his other arm he swept the parcel into his lap, hiding it in the pocket of his hooded overshirt.

After they had finished eating breakfast, John and Emily and Jimmy made their way towards the alcove where they had their secret conversations, a place that they referred to by saying 'let's go to play,' indicating that they should meet here to talk about something that they didn't want recorded, or overheard, by the Webispace.

Emily and Jimmy stood on the outside of the alcove, blocking any view from anyone who might be passing, and John stood on the inside as he began to unwrap the parcel. It was square, and hard, a few inches think, and several inches long.

"Someone has sent you a brick," said Jimmy, "that's really exciting. I'll have to remember to give you one of those for Ex-mas." In New Angle Land the old fashioned 'Christmas' had long since been replaced by a midwinter celebration that was known in full as 'Excellmass,' a celebration of everything excellent about New Angle Land. Most people called it 'Ex-mas' or 'Xmas' for short, forgetting its original meaning of a massive celebration of excelling.

"Wait," said Emily peering in more closely while maintaining her blocking position to prevent others from seeing what it was that John was doing. After the last piece of brown paper had been unwrapped, and fell to the floor in a little bundle of wrinkled detritus, like the skin of a walrus, or a particularly aged Elephant, John held in his hand something that was thinner and wider than a brick. It was less heavy too, though by no means light, and certainly heavier than even the most out-of-date thought pad. He turned it over in his hands. On the front was written something in faded letters that he could not quite make out. They were so used to being able mentally to turn up the lights at a mind command, which they dared not attempt to do in the alcove, that they were not accustomed to having to peer to see something in less than ideal lighting. Gradually, though, their eyes acclimatized.

"Lord…" Emily began.

"…Of the Flies," John continued. "It's a book," he said as he opened it and noticed the writing inside, writing that did not respond to his connection, or his thoughts, like the information delivered through a thought pad. The words just sat there, unblinking, unchanging, not scrolling, word after word, on page after page.

"There's something written there," Jimmy reached in and stopped John flipping through the pages, a card, two inches by five inches, fell out of the book. Jimmy picked it up and handed it to John.

" 'From a friend,' " John read, " 'The Truth will set you Free.'"

Jimmy and John were so entranced by this—the first book either of them had ever seen—that they had not been paying attention to who was walking past the alcove as they read these words. Fortunately, Emily, who had heard of books before and knew one when she saw one, had managed to keep guard and protect anyone from being able to see what was going on, for just then a voice of authority boomed from outside in the corridor.

"What are you three doing? It's time for class!" Dr. E.C. White tried to make his way into the little circle to see what was going on. Emily turned around and started to talk to him very fast, waving her hands expansively, so that Dr. White could not quite grasp what was happening behind her. John quickly stowed the unwrapped book, and the little card with the handwriting on it, back inside the pocket of his hooded overshirt. The brown parcel paper, though, was still on the floor when Dr. White looked in.

"What's all this? Making a mess?"

"We were just practicing mind frisbi with…paper," said Jimmy hopefully. Dr. White raised a quizzical eyebrow. "We figured if we could do it with paper it would be dead easy with a mind frisbi."

"Even you can't be that deranged," said Dr. White, "The object has to be connected to the Webispace for it to work, Mr. *Cowman*."

"It's Cowan, sir," said Jimmy.

Dr. White turned on his heels and started to stalk off, calling as he left them behind, "Class starts in five minutes! Don't be late!"

They were not late for class, this time, but it appeared that several other people were, though the Professor seemed to pay that no attention. In addition to the continued absence of Barry Dunlop, there were other empty chairs around the room where just a few days before the class had been full. No one said anything, and Dr. White made no comment and gave no explanation.

"We're going to have to find somewhere else to play," said Emily to John.

"Or keep a better look out," said Jimmy, trying not to look too shamefaced.

Dr. White connected to his thought pad, and all the remaining students did also, and soon enough his mentally projected explanation of E.N. Darrow's *Lessons in Logical Positivity* started to scroll through their minds. Darrow's principle of positive logic was given again ("The difference between logical positivity, and logical negativity is simple and essential: any resulting conclusion that puts down an individual cannot truly be deemed logical by the principles of logical positivity"), and when Jimmy looked rather bored a mental projection of two fingers flicking his ear lobe appeared next to him—much to the amusement of the rest of the class.

John was not paying much attention either, one hand connected to the thought pad, his other hand was touching the book, *Lord of the Flies*. Wary of his thoughts being read he disciplined himself to think of E.N. Darrow's positive logic, or failing that mind frisbi. But when he was back in his room, safely (he hoped) disconnected from the Webispace by standing in the middle of the room, wearing shoes, not sitting on the bed or leaning on his desk, he began to wonder what the book could mean by "Lord of the Flies," and what was the 'truth' that could set him free.

Chapter Six

THE TRUTH

Excited as John was to discover the truth, soon enough he found himself simply immersed in the book as a story. "It's really pretty amazing," he said one morning to Emily, "I found myself picturing what is being described—but not like in the Webispace where the pictures come from outside. These were my own pictures; they were things I was imagining and creating. It's pretty cool."

They were gathered as usual in their alcove, where they could meet to talk (they hoped) without fear of connecting unknowingly to the Webispace, and so having their thoughts read by any snoopers who happened to be prowling through the Webispace at that time.

"Where's Jimmy?" said Emily, looking around. They had arranged to meet there after breakfast that morning by saying that they needed to 'go to play,' their code word for a rendezvous in their alcove to discuss important matters that they didn't want Gayle College or the New Angle Land police to know anything about.

"I don't know," said John. They both were thinking about the recent disappearances of students at Gayle College. Just then a happy-go-lucky, tigger-like figure, bounded up behind them, his hair all askew, buckling his jeans as he walked and trying unsuccessfully to flatten down his wiry mop of curly hair.

"Sorry," said Jimmy, "slept in."

Emily punched him on the arm.

"We were getting worried," explained John.

"Besides," said Emily, "sometimes I think a good punch would do you the world of good anyway."

"Ow!" Jimmy exclaimed as Emily gave him another playful, but solid, thump on the arm, "Leave off! I'm not a punch bag you know!"

"John was just telling us how reading his book—what's it called, John?"

"*Lord of the Flies,*" said John.

"Well," continued Emily, "how reading his book is gripping his imagination."

"That's good," said Jimmy, stifling another yawn. "But what about this truth thing that that card told you would set you free? That might be even more exciting than ancient literature."

"I think ancient literature is very exciting," Emily protested.

"Yeah, but you think driving slowly and sensibly on the airway is exciting...whereas for most normal people..."

"Anyway," John intervened before Jimmy got punched on the arm yet again, "I haven't found any 'truth.' Not yet at least."

"Keep looking, mate," said Jimmy, "In the meantime..."

"In the meantime we had better get to class," said Emily.

Class that morning was in ancient literature. The teacher was Mrs. N.E. Waiye, a small grey haired woman, who wore half rimmed glasses over which she peered at John as he arrived with the others a few moments late. Her voice was shrill, which when it was agitated with frustration began to sound a little like an electric saw cutting through sheet metal, and even at its most moderate and calm was not exactly sweet as a bird song. Unlike Dr. E.C. White she did not gain control over her class by occasionally belittling the students, but her voice was so painful when she was angry that it was in everyone's best interests to keep her happy. Jimmy was never quite sure whether she realized that she had this effect on people—or whether her husband also did everything he could to keep her calm, or wore specially designed ear muffs whenever he had to disagree with her—but whether she realized it or not, and whether she consciously used it as a technique of control or not, it certainly worked. The rest of the class looked around crossly at Jimmy and John and Emily as they arrived late, and Mrs. N.E. Waiye screeched at them.

"Make sure you're here on time next class, okay?" said H. as he held his ears in his hands, rubbing them trying to get rid of the slight ringing sound inside with which they still reverberated after she had finished shouting at the latecomers.

The class in Ancient Literature began, as they connected by their thought pads to the Webispace, and Mrs. N.E. Waiye started to scroll over to them mentally the text they were considering, dramatized for them through the Webispace, a rendition of *Myths and Other Religious Experiences Textually Analyzed Line by Line* (otherwise known as M.O.R.T.A.L.L.). Right now they were watching as a man strapped on a pair of what looked like wings, with bird feathers and ropes, and began to flap off into the air, but as he flew up and up the heat from the sun melted his wing contraption, and he fell to the ocean below. Next was a picture of a man lifting a staff before a large river, and the river dividing into two and lots of people walking safely across, and then as they were followed by an army, the river smashing down together again and the soldiers being drowned in the water.

"Now," came Mrs. N.E. Waiye's sharp voice mentally projected to them through the Webispace. Everyone sat up with a jolt as the scratching sound of her tone hit them like a mind frisbi being scraped over glass.

"I don't know how she does it," Jimmy whispered to himself, "even over the Webispace. Quite an achievement."

"MR. COWAN!" screeched Mrs. Waiye, "YOUR ATTENTION PLEASE!"

"Alright, alright," said Jimmy, putting an almost comical expression of extreme concentration on his face.

"Now," Mrs. N.E. Waiye continued, "I want you to compare these texts from your MORTALL curriculum, with this," as she said 'this' a picture of Albert Einstein, working dutifully wearing a white suit, appeared before them, alongside his ubiquitous E=MC2 equation. "Einstein," she said, "Praise Be Upon Him, of course had to pretend at times as if he believed in god," the last word came out with a particularly painful screech, "but that was just because of the days in which he lived. He, of course, from his General Theory of Relativity, and the path of his what we now call New Angle Land Logic that you have been studying with Professor White, took us in a whole new direction, whose benefits we enjoy today. For your work this week I want you to compare and contrast these two M.O.R.T.A.L.L. myths of Ancient Literature with Einstein. Class dismissed."

"That was quick," said Jimmy as they left.

"Yes" said Emily, "but the work she gave us is far from easy."

"I wouldn't mind," said Jimmy, "if she would just keep her voice down."

"Did you notice," said John quietly, "that there have been no more disappearances from the class?"

"Yes," said Emily, "but did you notice that those who have disappeared are still disappeared?"

The semester at Gayle College continued uneventfully for the next month or so. John Broadus kept on reading *Lord of the Flies* in secret, in his room, and in their meetings in the alcove would update them on the latest chapter. At first he had thought it was going to be a nice sweet fantasy story, but as he kept reading the boys in the story started behaving worse and worse. He wasn't sure what the point of the story was yet, but it had gripped him, strangely, as no other Webispace projection invading his mind had ever managed to do. Somehow it was as if the story was not something forced upon him, but was becoming a part of him, something to which he contributed and was part author as well as reader by the imagination he offered which gave the story life inside him. There was no sign of any 'truth' yet though.

John was also showing increasing expertise in mind frisbi, to such an extent that he was now on his year's team, the first years who were, once selected, intended to play the second years, and then the second years play the third years. Never, at least not in the last twenty years or more, had a first year team won against a second year, and it was even rarer for a second year to beat a third year, but the matches were intended to stretch the teams so that by the end of Gayle College the third year was able to compete against other colleges around New Angle Land. John, though he was a firster and not from a family that had ever been to Gayle College before, and so had had no exposure to 'real' mind frisbi before, but only the computerized version that they saw on their first evening in the common room, was progressing remarkably fast. Everyone agreed—surprised though they were—that he deserved his place on the team.

They were not so sure about Labelle Malchance. She was not exactly terrible, but there was more than a little suspicion that she was there because the third year who was in charge of the team, Gerald Hawthorne, had decided that she was the best looking first year. Labelle did not help remove this suspicion by always turning up at the trials and the practices wearing the shortest mind frisbi skirt she could find.

"Looks more like a belt to me," said Faith Felicity once, to which Jimmy had replied, "But what a belt...," and thereupon been once again punched in the arm by Emily.

"Getting quite a collection of bruises there aren't you," said John, "you've got almost one for every season."

"If he doesn't watch out he'll have one for every day of the week," said Emily.

But despite questions about her ability, Labelle Malchance was on the team, as was Faith—who was actually a very accomplished player. Jimmy did not make it. Emily had not tried, nor had H. The other two players were two first years – Brian Eno, a short wiry individual with boundless enthusiasm, and Edward McGough, who had been selected because when he spread his arms his wing span almost covered the entire expanse of the goal. He was the "enforcer" of the team.

"Every team needs one," explained Gerald. "You can't allow yourself to be pushed around."

Nonetheless, that is exactly what happened as they lost their first game to the second years by the grand total of 43 to 1. John had scored the only goal, a remarkable double twist turn as the mind frisbi eluded the outstretched gasp of the second year trying to stop a goal being scored. John did not like to admit it but the double twist move had not been something he had planned; it had just happened, almost of its own accord.

"Still," said H. when he explained it later in the common room that evening, "you're the only first year to score a goal in the opening inter-year match for a long time."

"What do you mean?" said Jimmy, "They were hammered."

"They always are hammered," said H., "usually they also don't score anything. What John did was pretty impressive." He looked at John questioningly. "Even if he doesn't know how he did it."

Winter was starting to arrive at Gayle College, and Ex-mas, the midwinter celebration of all things excellent, was just around the corner. Soon enough it would be time for the students to return to their homes to enjoy the seasonal celebrations.

"Enjoy," said John, when he and Emily and Jimmy were discussing this in their alcove one rainy afternoon when mind frisbi practice had been cancelled, "Enjoy! I'd sooner enjoy a screeching match with Mrs. E.N. Waiye."

"What do you mean?" said Emily "Everyone enjoys Ex-mas."

"Not when you've got my parents, you don't. They think because I'm their only child I owe them something…frankly, it's a horrible experience."

"What's so bad about getting presents even if you don't like the people who gave them to you?" said Jimmy

"Of course you like them, don't you John. You've got to like your parents, haven't you?"

There was a pause as John tried to consider how to answer this question without sounding callous. It would take a lot of explanation for Emily to even begin to understand his so-called home life.

"Let's put it like this," said John finally, "last year at Ex-mas I did the cooking, I did the washing, I bought the presents, and I decorated the tree. It's like I'm the parent."

Jimmy and Emily looked at each other incredulously.

"I know it's not that difficult when you can connect to the Webispace to do the shopping, but some of that you still have to do physically."

"That's not what we were thinking," said Emily.

"We were thinking one of us should invite you for Ex-mas at our place," said Jimmy.

"I'm not sure my parents would allow that."

"Or at least," carried on Emily quickly, "the day after Ex-mas. We could have a proper celebration then. All of us could meet up at one of our homes. Come on, it would be fun!"

"That does sound fun," said John.

"It's a deal, then," said Emily. "I'll arrange everything."

"Do I get to play any part in this?" said Jimmy

"You, my friend," said Emily, about to give him another playful punch on the arm, as Jimmy moved swiftly out of the way, "Can be the life and soul of the party."

The idea of Jimmy being the life and soul of the party, or indeed the idea of any party, especially any party over Ex-mas, cheered John up no end as the semester wound its way towards Ex-mas holidays. Gayle College was preparing itself for the season by festooning the corridors with seasonal messages—"Merry Xcelling," one said; another, "May all your Excellencies come true."

As John read the word "true" on the way to lunch one day, it reminded him that he still had not discovered "the truth" which the card had urged him would set him free. He had kept on reading in *Lord of the Flies*, but as gripping as the story was, it had not yet revealed to him the truth. He sat down next to Jimmy and Emily, grumpily, touched the thought pad in front of him to order the food that he wanted for that meal, which momentarily appeared in front of him.

They were not in the Great Hall—where tradition maintained as yet no Webispace—but in the cafeteria for lunch that day, where food could be ordered through the Webispace and delivered to your plate without the need for moving. How the food itself appeared, John was not quite sure, but he gave it little thought as he dove into a plate of spaghetti.

"What's wrong with you?" said Jimmy. "Still not found 'the truth'? I'd give up if I were you, mate, and enjoy that spaghetti. Not," added Jimmy observing John eating, "that you need much encouraging to do that. Not been feeding you properly have we?"

"Don't talk about the 'truth' here," said Emily, "if we are to talk any more we should go and 'play'."

When they were in the alcove, away from the Webispace, Emily reminded them that while the Great Hall was normally thought to be disconnected from the Webispace, for reasons of tradition, every other space was not safe for unmonitored conversation.

"Yes Miss," said Jimmy, and wandered off to follow Labelle Malchance down the corridor. She had exchanged a short skirt for very tight jeans.

"How many changes of clothes does that woman have every day?" said Emily as she also left the alcove.

John left too, but as he did so he thought he heard the footsteps of someone walking rapidly away down the corridor. He followed the sound, but as he turned around the corner he only saw a group of second years examining a next generation mind frisbi. "Can't wait to throw this against you!" said one of them, looking towards John. "You might try catching it when you play. I've heard that helps!" as he said this he shot the mind frisbi towards John's head, who ducked just in time, as the rest of the second years laughed.

John carried on down the corridor. Once again he heard footsteps disappearing into the distance but fast as he walked he found nothing. He opened a door through which he thought he had heard the noise, and as he did so he found himself in the middle of a class.

"Ah, Mr. Broadus, can we help you?" the voice came from a teacher that John had not seen before now.

"I'm sorry professor, I must be in the wrong place."

"Actually, I'm not a professor, at least," the person at the front of the class room continued, "Not usually. My name is Ms. Meadows. I am the head of the Cognitive Police for the region in which Gayle College finds itself. I was telling the class," Ms. Meadows indicated the group of third years sitting neatly in rows, "about the danger of The Contagion. How it is spreading. And how we will not allow that to continue. Whatever the cost."

John did not know what to say.

"You may join us if you like," said Ms. Meadows. She tried to smile at him, but despite the attempt it looked more like a warning to John than an invitation. Ms. Meadows was a middle-aged woman, plump, whose rounded figure squeezed against the police uniform that John now noticed she was wearing.

"That's alright," said John, "I think I'll be off now."

John turned to leave, but as he did so, already half way out of the door, and the door about to shut behind him, Ms. Meadows called out, both through the Webispace to which she was attached, and loud enough so that anyone in the corridor would also be able to hear, "You already smell pretty off to me! Better go take a shower." Ms. Meadows laughed, and after a slight pause the rest of the class laughed too, hesitantly, trying to sound genuine. John waited a moment and then continued to shut the door, feeling lucky to have escaped with a little more than a backstabbing jibe.

He turned further down the corridor to arrive at his own class, where N.E. Waiye was already screeching her way through the next M.O.R.T.A.L.L. instruction, and slipped down into his seat.

Before he touched the thought pad he glanced around the room and noticed that now there were one or two new spaces missing. The class had started out with twelve, but now it was down to seven. He realized, with a jolt of shock, that Faith Felicity was not present. *Where could she be*, he wondered? She was never late for class.

The last day of school had now arrived, and Emily and Jimmy were saying goodbye and wishing each other a Merry Ex-mas. Jimmy was wearing an outrageous Father Ex-mas hat, while Emily was, more considerately, dressed normally so as not to make John feel worse about the lack of celebration to which he had to look forward. Emily and Jimmy's parents were waiting for them at the front of Gayle College, where John had been dropped off just a few months ago, a time which had seemed to race by so much had happened. John's parents were not there yet. They often seemed to leave him hanging around at these kinds of moments, as if to underline how undeserving he was of their attention.

"We'll arrange for you to come over after X-mas, at least," Emily said to John.

"Yeah," said Jimmy, "and if you are just given a pair of socks for Ex-mas then we can find you something fun to do. Remember," he said glancing amusedly towards Emily, "I am the life and soul of the party, right!"

Emily's parents smiled broadly at her from their mind car. *They looked like happy people*, thought John, hard working and eager to help Emily along her way. Every student had to be picked up by a parent (or guardian) according to New Angle Land policy, because ever since the wars of religion, the colleges, like Gayle College, were given especial responsibility to insure that the parents were on the same page as the institution. Before they could receive back their children, the parents had to complete a quick mind questionnaire at designated public thought pads at the entrance to Gayle College—a questionnaire intended to insure the essential soundness of the parents.

"I hope mine don't pass," said John, as they watched Emily's parents sail through the questions without any problems.

"It's never been known to happen, at least…" Jimmy carried on.

Emily interrupted him, as she hugged them goodbye, "At least not recently."

After a while, John was left on the steps on his own. Jimmy had gone with his parents, his father even more muscular and enthusiastic than his son if that were possible; his mother petite and pretty, which made John think that Jimmy might stand a chance with Labelle Malchance after all.

In his hand, inside his coat pocket, was the book, and in that the card that had told him to find the truth and that the truth would set him free. As he thought about this, he suddenly felt like he was being watched. He turned around, saw nothing, but once again over heard shadowy footsteps retreating around the corner of the entrance way to Gayle College. While John was sad to be so late to leave for Ex-mas, he felt he had little to look forward to, and he was more concerned with the continued, and unmentioned, disappearances of students. His class with E.N.

Waiye was now down to five. He missed Faith Felicity; she had still not reappeared.

He followed the footsteps. This time, as he turned the corner, he stopped, deciding instead of running after where he thought they came from, to try a different tactic. He placed his hand on the hard stone of the Gayle College entrance way, and mentally connected to the Webispace. He did not know that this part was wired for the Webispace, but evidently it was. Soon enough his mind was racing down the options immediately presented to him. He ignored them and concentrated on projecting into the Webispace the sound of the footsteps he had heard. He did not know if what he was doing was possible, but somehow, he thought, it might be.

Suddenly, in front of him, as it were, mentally projected to his right, was a blinking red light, as he looked into the mental Webispace it seemed to mark a spot. John disconnected and ran immediately over to where he thought the map had indicated, to his right, and inside a doorway that looked like it was a back entrance into the kitchens. As he opened the door there stood Gerald Hawthorne, the third year who was training them in mind frisbi.

"Don't be angry," Gerald said, stepping back from John's approach.

"What are you doing?" said John.

"Not here!" Gerald protested, wide eyed with fear.

"Here and now. I want to know. WHAT is going on?"

"You're being followed," Gerald admitted. "They've made me follow you. The mind frisbi can allow me access to your thoughts. They think you have a Contagion."

"Is that what happened to Faith?" John asked. "Where IS she?!"

"I don't know, *I don't know*," Gerald crumpled up into a ball as he slumped against the wall opposite the door. "Not here," he said, "Not *here!*"

"What's happened to them all, not just Faith but all the others. Where are they?" John insisted.

"They," said Gerald, looking away from John, "are gone."

Chapter Seven

WIDER COUNCIL EFFECTS

Emily Lee's home was near castle-like in size, John felt as he compared it to the ramshackle shelter that his parents provided for him. It was on the outskirts of a small village in New Angle Land, about a two and half hour drive from Gayle College, in one of the most prestigious residential areas, called Esmery Village. Emily's parents were doctors, not the professorial sort but surgeons. Her father was a brain surgeon and her mother operated on hearts. "After that," her father Dr. Lee used to joke, "you're on your own." Around the house were pictures of hearts in various stages of disease, and sections of brain labelled in detail. Emily told Jimmy and John that however early she would rise in the morning, growing up she would find her parents already awake, studying together in the small library off to the side of the kitchen, drinking coffee and discussing the day's upcoming procedures.

But it was the top of the house which really interested Jimmy. "That," he said, "is where the party should take place." Across the whole expanse, in scale what felt to be in total about half a mind frisbi field to John though in truth it could not have been quite so large, was one massive entertainment room. There were screens that appeared on the wall at the mental touch of a thought pad and would play anything you wanted, and project onto your mind a variety of layers of entertainment at once. There were other Webispace toys and techniques of various kinds, all chanelled to the mind connected to the thought pad at lightning speed, but the part of this room that really intrigued Jimmy were the old fashioned games. There was chess, not the mental kind with different layers of moves and counter moves, but the physical pieces, carved out of wood, chipped and worn through use. There was an old rocking horse, still there from Emily's nursery days, and which was on occasions being put to good use by Emily's two younger sisters, Grace and Trudy. It was by now quite late in the evening so Grace and Trudy were sound asleep in their rooms at the other end of the house, on the middle of the three floors, and were sufficiently far away to be undisturbed even by Jimmy's raucous behavior.

At that moment Jimmy raced back into the large expanse of the entertainment room from one of the side walk-in cabinets, clothed in even more outlandish clothes than the last time. He had a feather hat, a national New Angle Land replica mind frisbi jersey, what looked like pantaloons drawn from the fable of the Arabian Nights, and a mock scimitar. "Now, I will tell you a story!" he shouted as he spun around, and collapsed uncoordinatedly in front of John and Emily.

"Nice try," said Emily.

"I am meant to be the life and soul of the party. You said it yourself!"

"Yeah but I think the life and soul went out of this party about half an hour ago. Right after you burped for the fourth time," Emily turned away and made a gagging gesture towards John.

"Anyway," said John peaceably, "I've had a great time." He looked down at his collection of Ex-mas presents—none of them he noticed were socks. "Best Ex-mas ever. Seriously," he added towards Jimmy.

"Really?" said Jimmy.

"Yes, really. You've done a great job," said John.

"That's a relief," said Jimmy, taking off his outlandish hat. "I was running out of steam there I can tell you." Emily regarded Jimmy doubtfully as if she couldn't quite believe that however late it was, and however much partying he had been doing, Jimmy could ever quite manage to run out of steam, or feel like it was enough. "Besides," said Jimmy, "I want to find out what happened to John at the end of last semester at Gayle College. I'd like also to know what you got for Ex-mas from your parents too, mate."

"Don't bother," said John, "If you think it was socks you will think it was better than it was." Actually, that year John had been given a rhyming list of rules for doing cleaning and housework around his home.

A is for attitude: always work hard
B is for breakfast: never use lard

C is for cereal: nice and crunchy
D is for dishes: after every lunchy

John thought that his mother had made it up herself. It went through the whole alphabet and the rhymes (and the sentiments) did not improve as the list continued. The last pair was the worst:

Y is for you: never over fed
Z is for zzz sleep: go to bed!

He wasn't sure how they had made 'lunchy' rhyme with 'crunchy' and keep a straight face as they mentally projected the list over to him on Ex-mas morning, but the last two lines, though they worked a little better as a rhyme, had a message he appreciated even less. Especially when he compared it to the wonderful food, and the late night party, he was now experiencing at Emily's home.

"What are you thinking about John?" Emily asked, as she noticed his slightly glazed look on his face as he contemplated what he had received that year for Ex-mas. "Don't say anything!" she added, concerned that he might talk about things that they could only discuss when they were not connected to the Webispace. The entertainment room at the top of the house was certainly a lot of fun but it was the most webi-connected room in the house; if they were right about the Webispace being able to read their thoughts, they would probably barely have to give an idea a fleeting mental glimpse before it would be recorded, and monitored by any of the Walkers, the computerized drones, prowling the Webispace for epistemic thoughts, or signs of the Contagion.

Jimmy, Emily and John immediately realized the danger and buried any consideration of anything apart from the party deep inside their minds.

"Tomorrow," said Emily, "I'll show you somewhere else we can 'play.'"

The next morning Emily led the two friends out into the garden. "Not yet," she said as they took their first steps down the path. She pointed to the rocks on the path, beneath their feet, and they understood that even that might be wired for Webispace convenience. They carried on walking down the track, talking about this and that, with John trying to do a passable impression of someone interested in a garden. Jimmy raised an eyebrow at John as John said something about chrysanthemums.

"Ah," said Jimmy, "yes," noticing Emily's encouraging smile at this attempted conversation, "Nothing compared to a nice Winter Rose." Emily rolled her eyes, as they carried on walking. Eventually, they turned off the path and into a clearing, rather unkempt, that was surrounded by a small orchard of apple trees, and stood next to the compost heap at the bottom of the garden.

"Chose the best place did you?" said Jimmy, sniffing unappreciatively at the pong that was coming from the rotting vegetables.

"This is the best place to be away from the Webispace. Plus no one can see us," she said as they ducked behind the low hanging trees surrounding that portion of the garden.

"Plus," said Jimmy, "even if they could, if they had noses they would avoid coming here at all costs."

"Nice try about 'Winter Roses' Jimmy!" said Emily.

"Well, I had to think of something," said Jimmy.

"Perhaps you should stick to what you know next time," said John.

"Talking of what you know," said Emily, "tell us what you know about what happened at Gayle College at the end of last semester. You haven't looked yourself since you arrived, and this is the first chance we have had to talk."

John told them about what had taken place, and what Gerald Hawthorne had said to him.

"What do you think he meant by 'gone'?" said Emily.

"Dirty rotten scoundrel spying on us like that. No wonder we did so bad in our mind frisbi match against the second years. Other than you, mate," Jimmy said looking at John. "You did really well. The rest of them were a *disaster.*"

"Can we concentrate on the main thing," said Emily, "and I don't think they lost because of Gerald. They lost because— other than John—they weren't very good. The point is – "

"Yes Dr. Lee?" said Jimmy. They had been teasing her since they discovered the profession of her parents. "Would you care to give us your carefully considered expert opinion on the matter?"

Emily continued, ignoring him. "The *point* is what does it mean that they are 'gone.' "

"I don't know," said John, "He didn't say it like 'they are not here,' he said it like 'they are not here and they are not going to be here.' It was 'gone' like a balloon is gone when you let it go and it flies from your hand up into the air. It's gone and never going to come back again."

"Unless the wind currents change, or it's connected to the Webispace and you have really good mind control techniques, I heard of one guy once who…"

John interrupted Jimmy, "You get the idea. Gerald meant they were 'gone' gone, good and gone, over and out, done with, ended. That kind of gone." There was a pause while all three of them considered this. Then John carried on, "What I want to know is why has no one else mentioned their absence."

"Maybe they are too scared to mention it," said Emily

"Or maybe they are part of making sure they are gone," said Jimmy, turning serious for a moment. "If Gerald Hawthorne," he spat out the name with disgust, "was in on it, who else might be?"

With that uncomfortable thought in their minds, Jimmy and John and Emily spent the rest of the day looking rather forlorn, to such an extent that Emily's mum made an especial effort with dinner. "Best meal I've ever had," said Jimmy. "Makes all this almost worthwhile." Emily looked at him in a way to warn not him not to say, or think, anything further. Emily had not yet dared to mention anything to her parents about what was going on, and if she did she would have to find a way to do it while they were not in any danger of being connected to the Webispace.

That evening they went to bed a little earlier than usual, and John lay awake thinking about the fun he had been having in Esmory Village with Dr. and Dr. Lee, and Emily and Jimmy, and trying not to think about what it meant that the students who had disappeared were 'gone.' Eventually, he fell asleep.

Without warning, John found his mind mentally passing down the channels of the Webispace. No one had ever told him that this was possible, but this was now the third time such 'mental travelling' had taken place for John, and while it unnerved him just as much as the first time, this time he was ready and paid especially careful attention as his mind moved through the various channels and possibilities. It was almost as if something within him knew where he was going and what he was doing, even though his conscious mind was unaware and was simply watching and along for the ride. He took one turn, then another, until suddenly his mentally projected self stopped over what looked like a Cognitive Prison, one of the mass detention centers for those guilty of breaking the New Angle Land way. Twenty four hours a day, seven days a week, every single day of the year, these centers ensured that the individuals involved were mentally bombarded with New Angle Land directives, considerations, and positive logic. It was intended to reintroduce those who had been convicted of cognitive crimes back into society, though John had never met anyone who had returned from a Cognitive Prison.

As he watched, though, a highly unusual event began to take place. A mentally sealed prison door sprang open, a prisoner in solitary confinement inched his way out, others joined in as their doors to their cells also sprang open, and while John watched a mass breakout from the Cognitive Prison unfolded. The prisoners fought the guards, knocked some of them unconscious, gained control of the front gates, and while a few of the prisoners were shot as they fled a large number made it out of the prison and into the surrounding area. John had never seen a part of the countryside like it before, though he assumed it was a region of New Angle Land just one with which he was (thankfully, he thought) not familiar. It was desolate of buildings and habitations, and large, dense, sinister looking forests stretched as far as his mentally projected self could see. As he looked on, the prisoners ran for the forests.

Then his mind, switching from one side to another like your body does on a roller coaster ride at a fair ground, started to race down a different set of channels and possibilities in the mental Webispace. It was the Council chamber that he had seen before, deep in the Crypt of the Cathedral, and seated at the round table was the shadowy figure of The Chair, and around him sat the other members of the Council. John noticed that now there were several unoccupied seats at the Council.

"We have decided then," The Chair said, apparently summarizing a decision that had just been taken, "to take the more radical solution." A series of nods of grim determination went around the circle.

Once more John mentally shifted from one channel to another, he was beginning to feel quite worn out by the effort of this mental projection, and he raced down another track in the Webispace. It was at one of the call centers which were used to provide service for those who had questions about the Webispace, or needed help with some product or other. As usual, and as displayed in the commercials that advertized opportunities for work in such employment, there were banks upon banks of individuals, their right hands attached to thought pads, mentally answering questions from New Angle Land about the Webispace. And as usual all their answers were unfailingly polite, in accordance with policy and protocol, and without deviating an inch from the New Angle Land way, or New Angle Land logic.

A new group of workers had arrived. This group was being delivered, John realized, by the Cognitive Police. "More workers for you," the captain said to the supervisor of this floor of the call center. "They will be *perfect*," he said, "they are gone." They stood in three lines behind him. John's mental projection scanned down the blank faces of the individuals in these three long lines waiting to join the ranks of the call center, and to his horror he realized that he recognized some of the faces. They were the same people who had, moments ago it seemed to John but perhaps the time had been sped up as he viewed it through the Webispace, just escaped from the Cognitive Prison. "No more Contagion for you," the Captain said as each one passed under his watchful gaze through the doors into the training room for the call center.

"Have they been robotomized?" asked the supervisor of this floor of the call center, nervously scanning their blank faces.

"Perfect workers," said the Captain, "all Contagion gone, all epistemic possibilities gone, the perfect workers for your call center." He looked the doubtful supervisor up and down, noticing his hesitant expression. "Better than any robot, I can tell you."

The next morning after breakfast John suggested another walk in the garden. "Perhaps we can find your 'Winter Roses,' " he said smiling at Jimmy. They made their way in silence, despite John's attempt at humour it was apparent to the other two that something was troubling him. Emily Lee's mother had served up a breakfast sufficient to satisfy the most gluttonous, and even Jimmy was rubbing his stomach and groaning a little in a mixture of pain and satisfaction as they worked their way down towards the apple trees and compost heap at the bottom of the garden, where they were not connected to the Webispace.

"Puts you off your breakfast a little, doesn't it," Jimmy said, gesturing towards the compost heap once they had arrived and wrinkling his nose.

"Perhaps we should have brought you here *before* breakfast, then," said Emily laughing. "What do you want to talk about this time, John?"

John described what he had seen the night before. He had seriously considered not telling them, but the morning news, projected mentally if they chose while they were having breakfast that morning (Jimmy had been watching the replays of the national New Angle Land frisbi competition while John had been reading the news), described a mass break out of a well-known Cognitive Prison in the far north of New Angle Land. Apparently it was called "NALFAS" (the New Angle Land Facility for Acquired Socialization), the most prestigious Cognitive Prison in New Angle Land. No one had ever escaped before, the news report claimed, as it reassured the readers that all had been recaptured and returned to their cells, or died in a shoot-out as they resisted recapture.

"I think it must be true," he carried on. "I know it sounds crazy but I think I saw what *really* took place. They weren't recaptured, or some of them weren't, and those that were have been robotomized. They're now like drones in one of those sinister Webispace call centers. 'Perfect workers' the Cognitive Police captain said."

"Gives me the creeps," said Jimmy.

"I think it's time I talked to my parents about this," said Emily. "It's hard enough to find any time to talk to them about anything they're so busy. And I haven't found a way to get them far enough distant from the Webispace to have a proper conversation but I think we've got to try."

"How do we know," said Jimmy, "that they are not like Gerald Hawthorne. Meaning no disrespect," he quickly added, "your mum is the best cook since cooking was invented, and your dad looks like he has a brain the size of the universe, and your mum probably does, too, but we just don't know who is in on this and who is on what side, do we? Whatever being robotomized means I don't want it, thank you very much."

"We can't do nothing. And we can't ignore it. And we need more information. And we have to start somewhere with someone. I think we have to take a chance." John scratched his head as he said this. "Not that I think that talking to your dad is taking a chance, but I do understand what Jimmy means. Still, I don't think we have a choice."

"Jimmy?" Emily asked.

"Okay," he nodded in agreement, biting his lip. "Just next time bring me a bag clip or something so I can put it over my nose and I don't have to smell that pile of stench over there," he said pointing to the compost heap.

"Yes," said Dr. Lee as he walked down the garden path next to Jimmy, with Emily and John following on behind with amused looks on their faces. "That is a most intelligent question. Of course, as I can tell that you know, 'Winter Roses' are not truly roses at all, more formally they are known as 'hellebore' but like you I've always liked the name 'Winter Rose.' They flower even in the middle of a cold winter like this one. Actually they have another name too." Jimmy was trying to look fascinated as they kept on walking. Emily had suggested a late afternoon, early evening, stroll in the garden to her father on the pretext that Jimmy was fascinated with the garden and had made inquiries about 'Winter Roses.' Dr. Lee was now bending next to a plant that was amazingly in bloom even in the middle of the cold air. "You see," he said, "quite remarkable aren't they? And though they are not, of course, as glorious as a summer rose, when, like now, you cannot find anything else in bloom you can see why they were given the name 'rose' nonetheless."

"Dad," said Emily, "I wonder whether there might be any more of them down over there," she pointed in the direction of the small gathering of apple trees at the bottom of the garden.

"I don't think so, Em."

"I'd like to have a look anyway, *Dad*," Emily said. With a quizzical expression on his face, Dr. Lee followed Emily towards the apple trees, and went in behind them with her, with Jimmy and John following, to stand with them next to the compost heap.

"No Webispace here, Dad," said Emily meaningfully.

"You can't be sure about that Em, though you are probably right most of the time." He looked up at the sky above. "I can see no mind drones patrolling at this time, and I have heard no reports of them recently, but they are always developing new techniques to project the Webispace into unconnected areas. Still, I think we can safely say that we have some 'free air' at this moment right now. For a little while, at least. What is it that you want to say?"

"You tell him," Emily said pointing at John. "It's not like that Dad," she quickly added seeing the paternally protective look coming across her father's face as he scanned the boy, in his mind John was only a boy, up and down. "He's been seeing things. I don't mean that in a crazy way either," she said, "Oh, John you'd better explain."

John described the conversation he had had with Gerald Hawthorne at the end of the last semester, the disappearing students, including Faith Felicity, and then concluded by describing his mental visions, or projections, through the Webispace of the Council, and the call center, and the "robotomized" former prisoners. John looked down at the grass as he described all this. He was used to his parents treating his opinions, and experiences, with poorly disguised scorn and he was expecting little except at best a biting retort, or at worst angry derision. Instead, when he had finished, and he raised his head to look at Dr. Lee what he saw was not derision, nor even surprise.

"So you have discovered the truth," he said, "I wondered when you would find out," he directed this last remark to Emily. "I've been preparing you for it, and protecting you from it since you were born. I didn't realize it would begin like this."

"You," he said to John, "clearly have some unusual mental gifts. I've never heard of anyone being able to travel across the Webispace by their own mental projection and discover things, however much you appear unaware of how you do it."

Dr. Lee paused. "This could prove useful, but you need to learn to control it. It may save your life, and the lives of others, perhaps the lives of your friends who have disappeared. They may in fact, despite what Gerald claimed, not yet be 'gone' or robotomized. There may be still time for them. And there is certainly time for you three."

He looked affectionately at them all. "You see Gayle College is not what it once was, not what it was when I was there, Em." He trailed away as he looked off into the distance.

"Dad, what on earth are you talking about?" said Emily, "It sounds like you have known about this for a long time."

"We must carry on as if nothing has happened," Dr. Lee said quickly. "Our time here is limited. I think we can assume that this conversation has not been overheard yet, but if we continue here much longer the Walkers in the Webispace may become a little suspicious of just how interested Jimmy can be in Winter Roses." He smiled at Jimmy.

"You said they had another name, sir," said Jimmy. The other two stared at him. This time it sounded as if Jimmy was actually interested in the rose.

"Yes," said Dr. Lee. "They are also known as 'Christmas Roses.' Perhaps it is a good sign that our meeting took place here. They were called Christmas Roses because the story went that a child had nothing to offer as a gift at Christmas, and she discovered these flowers which she offered instead. I think we can take it as a good sign that good will come out of this conversation. But for now," he continued, "We must go back. You, John, must, I am afraid, return to your parents, and go about the rest of the holidays as normal, and then in due course go up to Gayle College. The best way to stay safe is to avoid any sign of what they call 'Contagion' or being 'epistemic.' They have quite enough of that on their hands already without worrying too much about a few more students."

"Is the Contagion that bad?" asked Emily.

"No," said Dr. Lee, "but now we really must go back to the house, and no more said about this then."

"Dad!" said Emily frustrated at the lack of information.

"What they call Contagion, I call health; and what they call epistemic, I call true knowledge. It is the body's, or the mind's, way of fighting a disease. It is a fever that we use to get rid of the lie. No more questions." With that he walked out from under the trees back up to the house.

Chapter Eight

ESCAPE

While the beginning of the new semester was not as startling as the end of the last one, for John even the most innocent events seemed to be increasingly filled with menace. He and Jimmy and Emily rarely made their trips to the alcove where they had thought they were always immune from the Webispace interference. After Dr. Lee's warnings, they realized that even such zones of free air could be overused, and become subject to suspicion. They rationed their visits there, and when they were huddled together they ensured that their time was brief. Emily had brought with her back from home a wind up, mechanical watch, which she used to time their meetings in the alcove so they would not go much over five minutes at once. And even such brief meetings were on a "as need" basis, rather than frequent and frivolous as before.

There was an air of intensity that John carried with him as he sat down to breakfast, then, one morning next to Jimmy and Emily.

They noticed his slight moroseness too, for they were also feeling a little wary, and on edge.

"What we need," said Jimmy, "is to do something to take our mind off all this hard work we have now we are in the second semester." Jimmy was trying to explain things that would not be interpreted as in any way possibly leading to a Contagion, or epistemic. As he said these words, Gerald Hawthorne sat down just a table away and looked over at them suspiciously. Somehow his old confidence had returned, and despite the encounter with John last semester he seemed not in the slightest bit scared of them now. Perhaps he had good reason to feel immune from whether they approved of him or not.

"What do you suggest?" said Emily, surprising herself with her willingness to consider whatever crazy suggestion Jimmy might come up with. Ever since Jimmy had showed an apparently genuine interest in "Winter Roses" (or Christmas Roses, as Emily would call them to herself when she saw there was no Webispace connection), she had openly wondered whether there might be a more serious, responsible, side to Jimmy's character. Jimmy, however, did not respond to her question; he was gazing off in another direction as if he had not even heard what she had said. She followed where he was looking. There was Labelle Malchance: she had come back from the Ex-mas holiday with a very dark tan, having been taken by her parents for a winter sun trip to the coast of the Islands of Everdales, a famed New Angle Land popular tourist area. Though it was still a little cold even now that the semester was starting to make its way towards the always delayed New Angle Land spring season, Labelle Malchance had dark glasses perched on top of her perfectly coiffured blond hair, and wore a sun dress that emphasized her athletic looking frame.

"I don't know how she does it," Jimmy was saying out loud, "She must be freezing poor thing. Perhaps if I go over and offer to give her my sweater," Jimmy started to stand up taking with him the dilapidated, faded and furry old sweater that he had shoved to one side as he sat down. Emily grabbed him by the arm.

"I said," she continued more loudly, "WHAT DO YOU SUGGEST?"

"Hmm?" said Jimmy, "Oh yeah right well. Something to take our minds off it all."

John smiled, trying not to laugh, as Jimmy attempted to return out of his dreamland to the reality around him. "You already said that," Emily said exasperated, "And then I said 'what do you suggest.'"

"And he said the same thing again, and then you said the same thing again. You two could keep this up for a while." John was almost laughing now.

Jimmy came back down to earth, "Right, well. How about a drive in my…I mean, my dad's…car?"

"Last time we did that I almost had a heart attack," said Emily.

"And I have to play in the next mind frisbi match with the second years right after this," said John.

"Well then how about when you're done," Jimmy said to John.

"Do I get any say in all this?" said Emily looking back and forth between the two of them.

"Nope," they said together.

John's mind frisbi match was not going considerably better than the last one. The second years, as usual, had far more experience and were therefore still outscoring the first years. The second years would mentally throw the mind frisbi to whomever was being marked by Labelle Malchance, and while she was the best dressed first year on the team without any doubt, her attempts at intercepting the mind frisbi were almost always forlorn. By this simple expedient the second years had managed to advance up the field and position themselves to score several goals in short order. Edward McGough, the tall lanky first year, would race back to cover the goal with his enormous arm span, but though he managed to block several of the shots, the sheer number of them that came his way through Labelle's ineptitude meant that before too long they were ten to nothing down.

"We can still do it!" said Brian Eno after the last score against them. He was bouncing up and down with wiry enthusiasm, like a terrier scenting a rat, or, thought John, like someone with more passion than common sense. It was true they were doing better than normal at this stage in the game, several times already John had almost scored, but almost scoring and actually scoring were two quite different things. As long as Labelle Malchance was in their team they might, like last time, get a consolation score but there was not much chance of them actually getting close to the second years, let alone beating them. Without warning, Labelle Malchance suddenly sat down. She reached forward and started to hold her right ankle, rubbing it up and down and moaning a little.

"I don't know," she said to Gerald Hawthorne who raced up to see what was wrong, "I think I must have just turned it the last time. I reached for that interception." She had actually flapped her hands inexpertly at a pass a moment before the last score.

"You have probably twisted it," Gerald said, placing his hand on her ankle and feeling to see where it hurt.

"Disgusting," said Jimmy to Emily, "look at him taking any chance to place his hands on Labelle. Who does he think he is. Just because he's a second year."

"You're just jealous," said Emily, trying not to look perturbed at Jimmy's concern for Labelle. "Perhaps I can help. I may not be a doctor yet," she glanced back at Jimmy, "but my parents did teach me a thing or two." She went over to where Labelle was sitting and confirmed the sprain, and helped Gerald assist Labelle as she hobbled off the field of play.

"Right," said Jimmy when Emily had returned to his side, "That's it then. It's going to be a massive hammering. They are down a man, I mean woman, now they really don't have a chance. As if they ever did."

John had gathered the remains of the team in the centre of the pitch. "Okay, I know that this means we are outnumbered but I think we have a chance if you do what I say." Brian Eno and Edward McGough looked incredulous.

Spikey Service, a red-haired student who had taken the place of Faith Felicity, spoke up, "We don't have any more reserves now I'm playing." This was the closest anyone had got to mentioning the disappearances, "so what do you mean we have a chance now?"

"What I mean is this…" John whispered some instructions to them.

As the play recommenced at Gerald's whistle, John stood out over on the left and the rest of the team ran to the right. This was not a typical formation. Brian passed the mind frisbi to John, cumbersomely as usual—other than Faith who was no longer with them, the rest of the first year's team were not even that good at passing, though Edward McGough was to be fair an impressive blocker of shots at goal. John caught the mind frisbi as the rest of the team ran far to his right in a little grouping. The second years stared at John, and then at the other players, confused and unsure what to do. John took the mind frisbi and then sent it skimming smoothly over to the group on his first year team to the right. The second years moved towards where the frisbi was, confident that they could either intercept it or mark them so that they could not pass the frisbi on again. As they arrived, however, the mind frisbi, with only a few seconds left on its control from John, shuddered, turned, and then skimmed back not to where John was, but to where he had run to, just a few yards from the goal. It reached him, his face circling on the disc, with the ten second control counting to zero, just in time.

He caught the disc and then while the second year students were still trying to work out how he had managed to do this, he propelled it into the goal.

A cheer went up from the first years, and the team raced back to be ready for their position. This time there was no Labelle Malchance, so though they were outnumbered they were able to intercept the mind frisbi and move back on to the attack again. Now the second years were not sure whether John Broadus would do a traditional passing move, or manage to boomerang the mind frisbi back to where it had come from and score in his unconventional manner. As the minutes ticked down to the final whistle the scores were ten to the second years, and nine to the first years.

"Here's my final suggestion," said John in their huddle before play recommenced with the second years holding the mind frisbi. As there were only a few moments left on the clock, everyone assumed that as usual the second years would win, though the first years had done much better than normal. John explained his plan while the others listened.

A big burly second year launched the frisbi to his teammate but just as it left his grasp something strange happened. The face on the frisbi switched to John's, then back again to the second years. John had done what Gerald had explained on the first day was possible: he was engaged in a mental battle for the mind frisbi, though this was much easier to do in practice, and they had only ever seen a third year do it in a competition with another college. The face shifted permanently to John's on the mind frisbi, spinning with a lurch and a shudder from the second year over to John, and John sent it careering through the goal at the far end just as the final hooter went for full time! The score was ten to the second years and ten to the first years! It was a draw.

The celebrations were soon almost getting out of hand. "How did you do it?" shouted Jimmy to John above the din. They were in the common room, which was now festooned with mentally altered slogans celebrating the achievement, and replays of the most memorable moments.

"It's only a draw!" said John, surprised by the sheer volume of the cheers that had greeted him when he had entered the common room.

"Only a draw!" shouted Emily as she joined the fray, "only the first time first years have not lost for about a couple of decades!"

Spikey Service slapped John on the back good naturedly as he marched over to the middle of the room to carry on dancing to the blaring music. Brian Eno and Edward McGough were engaged in a playful battle of mind arm wrestling—one hand was attached to a thought pad, while the other arm was engaged in a physical battle, and as the arm that was mentally projected battled so too the arm that was physically engaged battled as well. Brian was determined to win at least once, though John doubted whether that would ever happen as Edward slammed his wrist— both mental and physical—down onto the table once more. Though this was all fun, and John was despite himself having a good time, the sight of Spikey Service dancing reminded John of Faith Felicity whose place in the team he had taken, and that reminded him of the disappearances, and that made him fear for her. Was she 'gone' too? Whatever being robotomized meant he would not wish it on his worst enemy, let alone one of his friends. Emily was obviously thinking along similar lines as she too watched Spikey prance around good naturedly, and even the sight of Labelle Malchance coming into the common room on crutches (it was hard even for Labelle to look stunningly beautiful on crutches, though it certainly gave her an added sympathy effect on the male students in the room) could not quite cheer her up enough to forget all that had taken place recently.

"Come on," said Jimmy, walking back from the central dance floor area of the common room, "let's get out of here. Time for that much promised ride in my, I mean my dad's, car."

"Ugh," said Emily, "not that!"

"Great idea," said John, "you don't get a say, Emily, come on!"

The car roared into the air, up through the various lanes, and into the airway where Jimmy soon took the car into the fastest lane available, staying just below the speed limit. "Okay," said Emily, looking down at the bright lights of New Angle Land beneath, "this is not so bad, especially when you don't drive like a crazy walrus." Jimmy nodded appreciatively at that, though he gave John a broad wink when Emily was not looking and was once again staring dreamily down at the sparkling lights below.

"You want a go?" Jimmy said to John.

"Oh no!" said Emily coming back to herself and looking at John. "You remember what happened last time! My nerves are still recovering."

"John is in a much better mood now, aren't you John, more calm, more himself, it will be fine, won't it," Jimmy took the car out of the fast lane, across from the airway, down to the slower lanes beneath, and eventually to a stop on a ground lane all the way at the bottom of the New Angle Land air routes. "Over to you," he said, taking his hand off from the thought pad, and changing places with John.

As John got into the driving seat, he felt a strange tingly sensation in his hand, the hand that he used to attach to the thought pad. Brushing the sensation to one side, and concentrating on his driving, John took the car carefully and calmly up through the lanes and back on to the air way. "There, you see," he said to Emily, "more calm, more myself, see what I mean." John looked into the visicast that projected the traffic behind him and he noticed that coming out of nowhere were two police cars. "But I'm not speeding," he said confused.

"What's wrong?" Jimmy asked.

"I've got two police cars behind me, but I'm not speeding or anything."

"Better just keep going, ignore them, nice and calm," said Jimmy, leaning back in the car, trying to look as easygoing as possible so that Emily would get the message and not freak out. He was not at all sure why those police cars were there. They would not be following them for no reason.

"They are saying 'pull over,'" said John. A mentally projected picture of a Cognitive Police person with an arm raised had appeared across his mind, projected through the Webispace as his hand was attached to the thought pad, and the police person had said in a gruff, emotionless voice, "Pull over."

"I don't like that," said Jimmy.

"Nor do I," said Emily. "You're not speeding, Jimmy was not speeding. You're not doing anything wrong. It doesn't make sense.

Unless they are after something else." Even at that time, and in that situation, Emily did not want to risk mentally projecting all that they had discovered about the Contagion, about the epistemic mental virus, about the Cognitive Police, and the warning that her father had given her and them all over Ex-mas.

John was still thinking about this when he noticed that one of the police cars had actually sped up to drive right next to them, and the Cognitive Police person inside was looking across at him and now was physically gesturing for him to pull over. He was pointing across to the side, and down. His meaning was clear. He wanted John to drop down to the slower lanes and find a place to stop. John did not think he had much choice but to do so, as he noticed the armed fire power of the police, and the serious expressions. He knew that something strange was going on but at that moment he did not think he could do anything but obey instructions.

John started to pull over to the slowest lane on the airway, and then came off to go down to the slower lanes beneath, until eventually he was on a local traffic route and within a few hundred feet of actually stopping at the nearest park place on the ground of New Angle Land. As he was doing this, he happened to glance over not at the first car that had drawn up alongside him and gestured for him to pull over, but now at the other car which was hovering just to the other side of him at this point. Inside, at the back, was an older Cognitive Police person. It was Ms. Meadows that he remembered from his class, who had come to instruct third years on the Contagion. It seemed to John at that moment beyond doubt that they were being pulled over because they were now considered epistemic, that they had the Contagion. He remembered her biting sarcastic comment about him being "off" as he left the room, her leering gaze, and as he looked over once more at her small puffy petty eyes, he made a decision.

He floored it, in his mind's eye. The car jerked ahead of the patrol vehicles and zoomed back up to the interlane airway, going from the slow lane, to the fast lane, zipping back and forth in the most dangerous of ways possible. Faces of other drivers appeared on his mental scope, scowling at him and shaking their fists at him as he cut them off in a desperate attempt to get ahead of the police cars who were now following him with equal speed from below. Emily and Jimmy were too startled to say anything, hanging on for dear life, trying not to get thrown out of the vehicle. Their silence, though, John knew, gave unspoken approval to his actions. They too had realized that they were being pulled over because of the Contagion, though because John was the one doing the driving, at this point, at least, he was most culpable. As John continued to drive ahead, using the car like a mental mind frisbi, spinning it this way and that, bringing it crashing to a slower pace behind one car, and then jerking it forward again ahead of another, as he avoided the pursuing Police cars behind, he noticed that ahead of him, according to his mental scope, there was danger. The traffic was being commanded to slow down, as if there was an accident, and on every car's mental scope a voice was telling them to slow to hover speed. There was no way forward for John; the police had blocked his path ahead. He zipped off the airway, at the last exit before the blockage, careering down through the slower lanes, though hardly slowing his pace at all, with the two police cars behind him still in pursuit.

"It's me they want!" John shouted, unsure why he said this but certain he was right. Ms. Meadows had looked directly at him with something akin to triumph in her eyes. "I'll get you safely down and then I'll run for it."

"You can't do that, John," said Emily, frightened more than ever, "They'll catch you for sure."

"She's right, mate," said Jimmy, "And anyway where you go, we go. We're in this together."

John was not at all sure that they were, he wanted to protect them if he could, and he knew that his presence was bringing them into greater danger and difficulty than was necessary, but he was so busy controlling the vehicle as it drove at a herculean rate through the slower lanes, that he did not have enough mental energy to formulate an effective reply. He noticed, as he scanned beneath him for a place to escape, that there were groups of late Saturday night revelers piling out of the entertainment centres that now occupied the Cathedrals and chapels, in groups moving slowly into the still-used subways for mass transit beneath New Angle Land. In a moment, he took his decision.

Landing the car, haphazardly, not in a standard parking zone, but in the middle of a street, next to a bunch of revellers coming out of an entertainment zone, was no easy achievement, especially without causing any significant damage, though the people on the streets, some of them, screamed in shock as the mind car suddenly appeared in the street from above. Normally such accidents were prevented by the field of protection that invisibly spanned across New Angle Land, and beneath the air ways, so any debris, broken-down cars, and the like were caught in its stream and taken for refurbishment or disposal. Apart from at specific entrance and exit points there was no possibility of gaining access from above to the ground. John went down one of these exit points, but then screamed out of the parking zone, down the street to land ungraciously right next to the subway. Groups of people looked at them in shock, as two police cars followed close behind.

"I'm sorry," John said, disconnecting from the thought pad and hopping out of the car, "tell them it was my fault, blame me, tell them I captured you and made you do it, protect yourselves." And before they could protest, he was running off into the crowd, trying to hide himself in the mass of human bodies making their way into the subway.

The police cars drove up next to the car, and the Cognitive Police glanced briefly at Jimmy and Emily, but then, disappointed, looked around to see if they could find where John Broadus had gone. It was clear to Emily and Jimmy then that it was not them that that they were after. As soon as John had connected to the Webispace in the car through the driver's thought pad, the police had been alerted, and now he had disconnected they were looking for a new connection to locate him. They were only, if anything at all, mildly interested in Jimmy and Emily.

"My dad will kill me," said Jimmy looking at the car. But both of them were really trying hard not to think about John, and what might be happening to him.

Meanwhile, John was inching himself towards the subway, ducking in and out behind other passengers, descending on the ancient escalator to the trains beneath. As he did so he noticed the Webispace portals all around, for connecting to advertisements and train times, and predicting when the next train would arrive so minimal delays were possible. Studiously he avoided all these touch points, staying to the centre, and glad he was wearing non-webified clothing. He was not sure how he would enter a train without connecting at some point to the Webispace, but he hopped in behind an old gentleman who was travelling ahead of him, and managed to avoid any connection through the gate to the trains beneath. He looked behind him and caught the eye of a Cognitive Policeman. John wasn't sure whether he had recognized him or not, but he could not afford to take any chances, so he increased his pace, slipping between travelers for the late night subway, as the escalator continued to take them further down.

Unfortunately, John had been spotted. A shout came from behind, and as one of the Cognitive Police connected to a thought pad terminal for the police use, a rather unlikely picture of John appeared on all the mentally projected screens around them, a picture of him looking thoroughly 'epistemic' and subject to a 'contagion'. It had written underneath, "Warning: epistemic individual on the run. If you see him report immediately through Webispace to the Cognitive Police."

John hid his face further inside his hooded shirt and hoped, and hoped, he would not be noticed.

He turned with the crowd, and, then, out of the corner of his eye noticed a most amazing apparition. Stuck to the wall, mentally projected no doubt, but almost real, John thought, was a Winter Rose, what Dr. Lee had called a Christmas Rose. The other passengers ignored it, or did not see it, but it made John stop, oblivious for the moment to the dangers of the Cognitive Police catching up with him, or others noticing him and reporting him through the Webispace to them.

He knew full well that in his situation he should avoid everything to do with the Webispace, and avoid touching any surface that might unknowingly connect him to the Webispace through potential thought pads, but this Christmas Rose appealed to him. As he stood there looking at it, the lights all about him flashed once, twice, dimmed, and then a bright red spotlight shone down from above, focused on him, and outlined him to all those around him. On the Webispace screens all about him was suddenly projected the words: "Broadus located: Contagion in process of being contained. Do not move. Stand still."

Around him the passengers stopped and stared at John, some horrified, some curious. The mothers out late at night shopping hid the faces of their children protectively from seeing what was about to take place. Some of the younger ones who were more webified than others, fascinated by everything to do with New Angle Land, looked at him with an eager expression.

Within the red spot light a gas from above began to descend. It was still some way from reaching John, but John knew that it would affect his nervous cells and in one way or another render him unable to flee anymore from the Cognitive Police. He tried desperately to escape from the red light, now looking a little more like the harangued figure that appeared in the mentally projected Cognitive Police pictures of him, but found that there was no way out of the light. It was having a mentally restraining effect on him; he could not break through.

He looked once again, fascinated, at the Christmas Rose. He had moved close enough to it right before the red light had entrapped him that the rose was just on the outskirts of the light, almost, though not quite, within touching distance. As he stared at the rose, above it there appeared a picture of Dr. Lee, his face looking back at him eagerly through the red mist. Somehow leaping across the gap of the Webispace, inside mentally projected came words in Dr. Lee's voice, "Touch it," the voice said, urgently, "touch it."

John decided he had nothing to lose, as he looked back and saw the Cognitive Police descending the subway stairwell, drawing closer and closer to him, ready to bring him into captivity. He felt like a caged animal being given one last chance of reprieve.

"Touch it," the mentally projected voice said again.

John reached towards the rose, and this time, somehow, right where the rose was, as he reached towards it, the sinister red light parted beneath his hand and he reached through it and made connection with the Christmas Rose.

Immediately, it felt as if his body was being sucked out of one place and into another, as if he was being drawn speedily and unceremoniously down a water tube. The red light was gone. So was all light. It was dark.

Chapter Nine

DESTINY

At first Emily and Jimmy were too shocked to say or do anything. They sat there, the police cars hovering besides them, staring at the debris created by the car careering out of control down the street. After a while Emily noticed that Jimmy was stroking the side of the car with his left hand over and over again, rhythmically, repetitively. She wondered whether Jimmy had bumped his head in the sudden descent, or been hit by the car in some way or other as they had raced away from their pursuers. He showed no sign of stopping anytime soon, and so eventually Emily tapped him on the shoulder, and looked at him questioningly. He turned around and stared at her, his eyes wide with disbelief, "What," he said slowly, "will…my…dad…say…". Despite the severity of the situation, and this relatively trivial response from Jimmy, Emily found herself almost smiling at his misplaced sense of priorities.

"I think we've got bigger problems than your dad," Emily said to Jimmy as he turned back and continued patting the side of the car, lovingly, as if hoping that a little bit of tender care would put it back to how it was just a few moments ago.

In fulfillment of Emily's prediction, immediately a Cognitive Police person began to approach them. So far they had been ignored, while the Police ran after John. Assuming that he had been caught, Emily looked the Cognitive Police person in the eyes and, dispensing with her normal rectitude, said, "So you got him did you? Not content with forcing us off the airway when we've done nothing wrong, you so frighten the driver that he takes off on foot into the old subway beneath New Angle Land, and then you chase him down there like he's some common criminal. Who do you think you are? Don't you know we're students at Gayle College, and come from old New Angle Land families." She knew this last part was not true of John, but it was defensibly accurate with regard to Jimmy, and it was certainly true of her at least.

The Cognitive Police person stopped beside the car and said nothing at first. He touched the mobile thought pad on his wrist with which elite police and military commanders were equipped, and then said to them both. "Wait. Your turn will come."

Eventually, sitting in the car, in the open air, watching the Cognitive Police search for John, calm down the crowd, clear off the debris, and return the street to normal functioning, Emily noticed that it had started to rain.

"Great," said Jimmy, "just what we need. Not only will my dad kill me, but I'll catch a cold as well. I hate to do laundry," he added, realizing that this sequence of events was not quite making sense. "Anyway," he continued quickly, "The only thing that would make this worse is if we were at the bottom of your garden standing next to that blessed compost heap."

Emily realized that Jimmy was trying to make light of the situation, and that he had not actually lost his mind as she had first thought. She smiled at Jimmy encouragingly. People responded in different ways in times of crisis, she realized; perhaps this was his way of coping. Perhaps he was trying to help her cope, and as unhelpful as she found his attempts at humour, she thought it would do him good for her to at least look as if she was showing appreciation for his efforts.

"Eyes front," the Cognitive Police person said, and as Jimmy and Emily followed his direction, they noticed that standing at the front of Jimmy's father's now rather dilapidated vehicle was a woman. It was Ms. Meadows.

"Isn't that the Cognitive Police captain who comes in and gives lectures to the third years about the Contagion?" said Jimmy, not daring to take his eyes away from Ms. Meadows' ample figure. Her impressive girth, despite the extra coverage which her rain overcoat afforded, was obvious enough even to those who had not seen it before without a coat. Her frame pushed against the edges of her clothes like a well inflated balloon, but not filled with air, certainly not lighter than air helium, but a heavier substance, water, thought Jimmy, or sand, or even porridge—the balloon of clothes was filled but in a lumpy way.

"You two," she said, "have some explaining to do."

"At least," said Jimmy, "we don't have any homework to do—I hate New Angle Land logic; now a nice bit of explaining sounds like almost a rest." Emily could not quite believe that

Jimmy was managing to keep a running commentary going while they were being brought in for questioning by the New Angle Land Cognitive Police. The situation could not be much more serious, thought Emily, but Jimmy was managing to describe it as a fun day out. Ms. Meadows simply ignored Jimmy, gestured to the Cognitive Police person standing next to her, and Jimmy and Emily found themselves being directed into a Cognitive Police car.

"What about my, I mean my dad's, car?" said Jimmy, sounding serious for the first time. Ms. Meadows just rolled her eyes, and Emily and Jimmy were bundled into the rear of the car. It took off into the lower lanes, and made its way up until it reached the airway again. "I always did like going for a drive," said Jimmy, back to trying to cheer up Emily (and himself).

Before long they realized that they were not being taken to the New Angle Land police compound but were returning to Gayle College. The same thought occurred to Jimmy and Emily as they noticed the direction in which they were headed: Perhaps they had not caught John after all. And even if they had, somehow there was not enough evidence against them to warrant taking them away from the supposedly protective environment of the elite Gayle College. This felt comforting, though quickly Emily remembered that being at Gayle College had not prevented students disappearing, or being considered part of the Contagion, yet at least they knew the college and it felt as if they were in less immediate danger.

They were taken into the classroom where John had first seen Ms. Meadows teaching a group of third years earlier in the year. This time the classroom was not full, in fact it was empty apart from Ms. Meadows already sitting in a solitary chair at the front of the class, oozing over the sides like treacle over a sticky bun. There were two chairs opposite her, evidently intended for Emily and Jimmy. They were pushed down into the chairs by the two Cognitive Police who had accompanied them from the car to Gayle College, and now retreated behind, just out of their vision. Emily and Jimmy looked forward and found Ms. Meadows smiling at them, or at least doing what she evidently expected them to think was a smile but was more, Jimmy thought, like an expression you would find on a constipated baboon than a happy friend.

"Now, dears," said Ms. Meadows. "As you can see we are all friends here. We've brought you back to Gayle College, and after you've answered a few questions we can return you safe and sound to your common room, or to your own rooms, and you can go on with your lives just as you please."

"Where's John?" said Emily, surprising herself with her bravery. Jimmy turned to her, astonished by her direct approach.

"What she means is," said Jimmy doing what he could to keep things calm, "it's a nice day for a drive don't you think?"

"Mr. Broadus' location is none of your business," said Ms. Meadows, ignoring Jimmy with a dismissive wave of her podgy hand. "What you need to focus on is answering my questions." She said the word 'questions' with a sing-song lilt, as if it was intended to ease any concern that they might have, but really made Emily feel sick, the feeling you get when you have eaten too much ice cream, or when someone does something inappropriate or unfitting like cheering happily when someone has lost or failed. "You will notice," Ms. Meadows continued, "That I am not connected to the Webispace, and I have moved your chairs away from the Webispace portals in the desks in this room. I want to give you the opportunity to answer my questions without resorting to mind control techniques of inquisition, which can themselves be dangerous," the last word she said also with a smile, but this smile was genuine. The idea of putting them in danger seemed to give her pleasure, though for the moment she was, she had been indicating, foregoing that opportunity. "Now," Ms. Meadows said when a chill had entered the room at the word danger, "My first question is this, 'when did John Broadus first manifest signs of the Contagion?'"

"That's like asking someone 'when did they first start beating their wife,' " said Emily, who had been trained to think with ancient ways of logic by her parents. As she thought of her father she remembered his advice to be careful when they had last spoken without being spied upon by the Webispace in their garden over Christmas, and so she prevented herself from saying anything else. She had wanted to question the whole idea of a 'Contagion' but realized it might not be prudent.

"Remember, my dears, I can always reattach you to the Webispace." There was a pause as both Jimmy and Emily considered what sort of techniques the Cognitive Police might have to probe their minds. "Maybe you, my boy, will be more sensible. I will ask you the same question: 'when did John Broadus first manifest signs of a Contagion?'"

"Actually," said Jimmy quickly replying, "That's not the same question. Previously, as you may remember, you had said it was 'the Contagion' this time you said it was 'a Contagion.' " Jimmy was also thinking of how Ms. Meadows might be able to probe their minds through the Cognitive Police techniques of interrogation. "Anyway," he carried on determined to do what he could to protect his friend, "don't know what you're talking about, do we Emily?"

"That's right," said Emily, "no idea."

Ms. Meadows motioned to the two Cognitive Police people behind Emily and Jimmy, forgotten while they had come face-to-face with Ms. Meadows, and they stepped forward with portable thought pads, strapped them to their left wrists, and locked their hands onto the pads, palm down, so they had no choice but to make contact. Ms. Meadows connected to her police thought pad on her arm, and immediately her mentally magnified voice appeared in theirs. "So, then, let's do it this way. Can't say I didn't warn you."

Emily felt her mind pushed to one side, and locked inside a mental prison, while she watched as Jimmy's mind was explored for memories of John, and thought patterns that could be associated with the Contagion. Jimmy did what he could to fight the intrusion into his mental space, an intrusion that was meant to be neither possible, and if possible, certainly not legal. She looked across and noticed a picture of a book, with the title *Lord of the Flies* emerging out of Jimmy's mind, and then a piece of card with a saying on it "the truth shall set you free." Jimmy was then in his turn locked inside a mental prison, his mind pushed to one side, and her mind was then explored, vigorously, painfully. It felt like a hot rod was being thrust into her cerebral cortex; the agony was so extreme that she was surprised that she had remained conscious, even though she knew that nothing physically was changing, mentally she felt unclean, unwashed, exposed. She fought Ms. Meadows and for a while all she could see were mental pictures of mind frisbi games and New Angle Land logic classes, and then, though, after a brief fight came the same images of the book, *Lord of the Flies*, and the card saying "the truth will set you free." Exhausted, she slumped back against her chair. Out of the side of her vision she noticed Ms. Meadows nodding towards the Cognitive Police who detached her and Jimmy's hands from the thought pads.

"They will be fine," she heard Ms. Meadows saying. With her last remaining energy she opened her eyes a crack and saw there was a man in the room, a teacher. "No permanent damage. I did warn them but they were trying to be brave. Sweet really," Ms. Meadows was saying patronizingly. "Still, as I say, they will be fine. They will wake up with a very bad headache that's all."

"I don't want their parents to cause trouble," with a start of recognition Emily realized that the voice belonged not to any professor but actually to the president of Gayle College, Gary E. Dreyfus.

"Leave their parents up to me," said Ms. Meadows. With that, Emily could not retain consciousness anymore and passed into a painful dreamless sleep.

It was dark. John, having spent all his life in New Angle Land citiscape, had never really seen dark before. Even at night, when the lights were turned off, there was always light coming from somewhere, street lights, city lights, building lights, lights from above as the airway roared across the skies twenty four hours a day seven days a week. This was dark like no dark John had experienced before. He could not see the hands at the end of his arms; however much he blinked it did not get any lighter, and his eyes seemed to adjust whereby he could barely make out a finger if he held it close to the end of his nose but when he stretched out his hand again it disappeared into the darkness. It was not pitch dark; it was the darkness of which the insides of rocks are made.

But not only was it dark, it was quiet. John had spent every moment either directly attached to the Webispace, or about to be attached to the Webispace, or within near connection to the Webispace. When there was not noise outside from the millions of New Angle Land there was always noise projected inside, from the countless streaming conversations and music and games and entertainment and news filters of the Webispace. His mind searched for some input, audible or mental, and discovered there was none. For the first time in John's life not only was it dark, it was also quiet. He was left alone with his thoughts.

This womblike existence continued for some time, though unlike the child in a womb John could not feel a beating heart of a mother or kindly muffled voices of parents. Still, quiet, dark, John began to think. He realized that his mind, long used to responding to input, could generate ideas and pictures all of its own. It took some practice, but gradually, and very imperfectly, John began to experiment with creating a picture in his mind of the *Lord of the Flies* book that he had left in his room. He knew he was not connected to the Webispace, so he had no fear of being spied upon by the Walkers, and given that he had been chased down a subway he realized that he was under suspicion already even if he was connected to the Webispace. As he thought on his own, without intrusion, or intervention, or input, from outside, he was able to see the *Lord of the Flies* book, and see the page number which he had last read. It was almost as if his mind was being reborn.

It was hesitant; he would conjure up a picture of the card with 'the truth shall set you free' written on it, and for a while see the writing on the card, and the size of the card, but then momentarily his mind would be unable to hold the picture for long and it would disappear again in confusion. But the longer he tried in the dark, and the quiet, the easier it became. His mind was moving from being a consumer of mental projections to a producer. It was a strange transition, and he would have made no progress at all if he had any choice in the matter. But with each failure to generate a mental picture, or thought from within, there was an extended dark, silky, silence, in which John could hear nothing but the beating of his own heart, and in such quietness eventually something from within decided to try again. He started to imagine what might have happened to Emily and to Jimmy. He reached with his hand, spontaneously, as if he could connect to a thought pad to search for them, but realized that in the quiet, and in the dark, there was no thought pad, only imagination. Possibilities came to his mind, options that would present themselves to his friends, arrest, capitulation to the New Angle Land way, brave resistance, perhaps, he realized with a frozen horror, robotomization. At that word, appearing in his mind, self-generated at that point, John began for the first time to not only think but to think for himself about what that word could mean: 'robotomization', clearly not good, not normal, not nice, but what did it mean? Were they making humans robots? Were they somehow changing the mental capacities of humans simply to make them more efficient for the economy of New Angle Land? Was it necessarily such a bad thing if people were made to enjoy work which if they were left to themselves they would hate, but still have to do? Again, John could not hold such thoughts in his head for long—in the same way that he could not hold the mental pictures in his head for long either—but with each failure, came a long, silky, empty silence, broken only by a thud-thud of his own heart, keeping time with the lengthy intermissions of active thinking and imagining. After a while, again, John found that his mind, almost of its own accord, and unprompted, and uncluttered, by Webispace invasions, was actively engaged in thinking, imagining, creating, and being. The last was perhaps the most surprising to John: sometimes having thought for a while he would stop and contemplate his being, his nature, his 'his', the 'I', the self. Something inside was almost becoming angry at the realization that he had had little time to develop his own sense of what he liked, and did not like, what he preferred, and what he preferred never to see again, his tastes, his joys, his disgusts, his pleasures. The dark, and the silence, began to be filled with him himself.

Because it was so dark, John had not yet dared to move in any direction or the other. As far as he knew he could be standing at the top of a cliff, or alongside an edge that would fall down even further beneath the ground (he assumed he was still a long way down, perhaps even further down than the subway). After he had been testing his mind against the silence for what seemed like a long time, but really only a few moments so much more time did John have when he was uninterrupted by the Webispace, he reached out a hand to see if it would connect to any wall or surface on either side. With his fingers sprayed he touched what appeared to be a wall on the right. He reached with the left and found nothing, as he stood there. Deciding therefore to stay close to the wall he inched along it with his feet feeling their way out each step, hesitant, unknowing whether he would find an edge, or a barrier, or some obstruction, or something worse at any point. He continued creeping along the side of the wall, dark as ever all around, silence except the scraping of his shoes shuffling along what he supposed was the floor, or the ground, when suddenly to his right, where his hand was feeling there was nothing. He stopped immediately; the wall, as he called it, was no longer there. It was just an empty expanse, he turned his head slightly to the left as once more he felt with his left hand on that side to see if now there was any wall or guide that he could use to take him a little further away from where he had come, and perhaps find a way out. As he turned to the left, a hand from the right grabbed his arm, at the top, near the shoulder, and pulled him to the right. He fell, and then was caught by what felt like several pairs of hands. He struggled, not knowing who had pulled him, where he had fallen, or to what people these hands belonged, in the dark, friendless night.

"Shh," said a strangely familiar voice. "Say nothing. Think nothing. You are safe, for a while." John was raised to his feet. His hand was placed on the shoulder belonging to the voice who had just addressed him. "Keep your hand on my shoulder and follow carefully," another hand rested on his shoulder from behind. "We will stay in line until we arrive."

"Arrive where?" John found his throat cracked, and dry; he was thirsty with anxiety, he realized, now he spoke for the first time.

"You will find out," the voice, which John could not place but thought he recognized—or was it a trick of the eery darkness so that any human connection was viewed with potential hope?

They began to shuffle forwards once more. After a long time in this slow, snake-like, journey into the furthest darkness, surrounded by silence, except for the noise of an occasional scrape of shoe against floor, or muffled breathing, the voice ahead called, "Stop." A light flickered: it was a flame, not electric, certainly not Webispace, but an actual small fire at the end of a tiny piece of what looked like wood. The flame was moved to the side, where it lit a larger fixed stick, which John realized was a candle, but not a candle as he had seen countless times on the Webispace, or the electronic versions of candles that you would find in homes. This was a real fire atop an actual wax candle. "We are here. Wait."

The man walked ahead, taking with him a candle, and gradually lit others around the room, until he came to a fireplace at the far side. He bent down and lit the fire, which slowly began to burn, and then throw a flickering, warm light against the walls. As John's eyes became accustomed to what at first had seemed like brilliant light after the lightless dark before, he observed there were several chairs in the room. He counted them: twelve, as there had been twelve chairs in the Council where he had found himself mentally transported those two times. Except these chairs were not expensive looking, or formal, but a strange assortment of old comfy seats, and deck chairs, and arm chairs. They were arranged not around a polished oak board room table but in an open half-circle, with the fire now gaining strength at one end. John realized that what he had thought was a large group travelling with him was really only two people, one who had gone ahead of him, and one behind him. There were two empty chairs in the semi-circle of this room, seats that evidently belonged to those who had brought him to this place, wherever it was, and for whatever purpose.

"Welcome, John," the voice that had led him here said, friendly and genuinely. "You will see that there is no Webispace here, not even any electricity, for fear that someone might discover a way to use that means to transmit Webispace to this location. The Webispace can be used for good, but at present it is dominated by the Council, and its minions, and every thought is potentially read by the robotic Walkers who patrol its corridors. Here we can think, and speak, our minds, without fear of our thoughts being recorded and used against us.

"You will notice that there are twelve seats, much like the twelve that you saw in the Council chamber, which secretly exists beneath the Central Cathedral entertainment complex in New Angle Land, and to which I believe you were mentally exposed." John was not sure how the speaker knew this. "Yes," he carried on, noticing John's surprised expression, "Your," he waited for a moment, "unusual abilities with the Webispace have been noted, and not just by the Cognitive Police but also by us. We must admit that you have arrived at this point earlier than we thought…"

"And not at all by my advice," came another voice from one of the chairs.

"As you can see," said the first speaker, "we are free here to speak our minds, and think our own thoughts, and it is probably time that you were introduced. This, John, is the Underground. We are all that remains of Freedom in New Angle Land." John could not still see the features of the main speaker of the group, with the flickering candlelight making clear vision difficult and, he realized, each of the members of the Underground twelve wearing hoods over their faces, and not facing him directly.

"Unlike the Council that you observed, we are known to each other, though we keep our identity a secret to others. Nonetheless, for you to play your part in the unfolding drama ahead of us, it is necessary that you are brought into the group...eventually. Not now."

"And forever if you do not pass," said the same voice that had spoken against the main speaker previously.

"Yes it will be necessary for you to develop...wisdom...before you can see our faces, or know our identities. It is not that we do not trust you, John, but that when back on the outside again, back up there," he looked up and once more John thought he caught a glimmer of recognition from his voice, and this time from his shadowed facial features, "you must be able to hide your thoughts from the Webispace otherwise all of us would be unmasked before the true Contagion."

"I thought..." John began, "I don't understand I thought they were worried about me having a Contagion."

"You do have a Contagion, John," said the speaker, "but not the one they say you have. It is the beginning of health, for despite your astounding natural mental abilities with the Webispace it is not the same as being wise. We made sure you received that book, with the card, and gave you the idea of looking for the truth. That search is not a Contagion. It is the first step to cure. But you are not yet cured. We must cure you before you can help us bring freedom to Gayle College."

"And," this time a woman's voice speaking for the first time, "the rest of New Angle Land."

"Not yet," said the speaker again, "it is too soon to overburden the lad. First we must find a cure for him. He must start down the path of wisdom."

John did not know what to say. In the last few hours he had gone from being an easy going student at Gayle College to being chased by the police in an airway speed crash, rushed down into the subway, being somehow moved physically—how he still did not understand—through what looked like a mental portal, transported to a dark, utter dark, place. And now this, this 'Underground' were about to administer a cure.

"How do I know I can trust you?"

"You don't, but you will find that you can. Besides it is not us you need to trust. It is the truth. You will find it has its own trustable quality to it. In fact," said the speaker observing John carefully, "I think you are already discovering that to be the case. It is not a case of trust; it is a matter of truth."

"Why me? Why I am here?"

"We have been watching you, John," the speaker who had spoken a contrary opinion now sounded friendly towards him, if cautious still nonetheless.

"Yes," said the main speaker, "indeed. You are most unusual, John, most unusual. You can do things in the Webispace that even some of our best advanced students cannot yet."

"Eh-hem," another voice coughed as the main speaker mentioned students, apparently concerned that more of their activities were being given away than was necessary at this point.

"Even," carried on the main speaker, "even things some of us struggle to do with regularity. Though, as I say, you have much to learn, you must begin to be, at least start to be, wise. That way you will have control of your abilities. And without it, you will be still too infected to be anything but a danger to Freedom, to us, and even yourself."

"What must I do?" said John, not sure if he trusted them yet, but wanting to find out precisely what they were suggesting.

"You," said the main speaker, "must learn to think."

Chapter Ten

UNDERGROUND

It was not until the next day that Jimmy and Emily found a moment to review what had taken place.

"Splitting headache," said Jimmy, as they snuck back into the alcove where they hoped that their conversations were at least for the most part unobserved and unwatched through the Webispace.

"What I want to know is," said Emily, rubbing her forehead a little as well, "how does she get away with it? I mean with all these disappearances, no one says anything, if they notice which I don't see how they couldn't, and then she treats us like that, and the president doesn't do anything about it. And then here we are going about Gayle College as if nothing happened."

"Perhaps everyone else is scared," Jimmy suggested. He had switched from rubbing his forehead to rubbing the back of his neck.

"What do you mean 'everyone else'?" said Emily, "I'm scared too. But it's not going to stop me doing something about it. Listen," Emily continued, looking over Jimmy's shoulder to see if there was anyone walking down the corridor at that precise moment, "I have an idea."

Later that day, during mind frisbi practice for first years, Gerald Hawthorne was as usual enjoying bossing everyone around. A diminutive first year had taken John Broadus' place in the practice team, while everyone else carried on us as usual as if nothing untoward had taken place now that the star of the game the other day was no longer there. His name was Barry Bright, and though he tried hard, and was not as bad as Labelle Malchance (who seemed to have made a full recovery from her injury and was now playing as well, or as poorly, as ever), he still was no replacement for John. The team went about their practice in the central court area, the quad, of Gayle College, without much coordination or enthusiasm—other than from Gerald who delighted in pointing out their mistakes. "You'll never win a game like that!" Or, "Just because you drew the last game doesn't mean you're any good, you know. It was pure luck! It'll never happen again." Or, when Labelle Malchance passed a very slow mind frisbi to Barry Bright, who failed even to catch it in his eagerness to pass it quickly on to Brian Eno, he just guffawed, chortling into his hand without much attempt at hiding his amusement at their expense. "Right," said Gerald, "practice over. Remember, they say practice makes perfect...or in your case...not," he smirked to himself as he wandered off towards the Great Hall.

Jimmy and Emily followed behind, talking to themselves about the weather.

"Nice day for a spot of mind frisbi, don't you think?" said Jimmy. Emily tried to keep a straight face at this rather poor attempt at normal conversation.

"Eh, yes, absolutely, glorious, I agree," Emily replied.

At this point Gerald turned around and noticed that they were now right behind him, a little closer than might be typical. "What are you two doing? Are you following me?"

"Oh yes," said Emily, thinking quickly, "we were just talking about what wonderful weather it is for mind frisbi, and I was wondering," Emily put on her most winsome smile, "if you could tell me what it's like to play in really bad weather, say when you're playing a serious game like against the third years or something, that must take a lot of strength, and courage," Emily fluttered her eyelids at Gerald. Jimmy looked across at Emily unable to believe that such an obvious bit of flattery, however pretty Emily was trying to make herself look as she flicked her hair back from shoulders, would work on Gerald.

"Oh well," said Gerald, "follow along then. I can tell you whatever you want. I suppose you can come too," this last comment was spoken to Jimmy, as if Gerald was now hoping that he might explain the finer points of mind frisbi in a personal *tête a tête* with Emily in his *boudoir.*

"Come along Jimmy," said Emily quickly, "I want you to hear how amazing he is." Emily steered Jimmy alongside her as they followed Gerald a little further down the corridor, Gerald mollified at the thought of Jimmy's ongoing presence by the idea that he was there to witness how remarkable a person Gerald was.

Emily was carrying on a continual conversation about weather, and mind frisbi, and how to spin it this way and that, all the time sounding interested and fascinated, while they drew closer and closer to the alcove where Jimmy and Emily knew they could talk without being exposed to the Webispace—at least they thought they had managed to do so thus far. As they passed the alcove, Emily looked at Jimmy, and Jimmy shoved Gerald into position, grabbed him by the arm and spun him around to face Emily who was now blocking the entrance so no one could see what was going on.

"Now," said Jimmy, "we have some other questions for you."

"Yeah," said Emily, no longer fluttering her eyelashes or flicking her hair, "and they're not questions about mind frisbi. For a starters…"

"I heard what happened to you," interjected Gerald, looking surprisingly unconcerned by their interrogation.

"What do you mean?" said Jimmy.

"I mean about you and the Cognitive Police, and Ms. Meadows," Gerald was evidently better informed about what was going on, somehow or other, than either Jimmy or Emily had predicted. "You can't hurt me. You're in trouble. You're going to disappear, that's what I think anyway." Jimmy and Emily looked at each other, wondering whether there was any truth in what Gerald was saying, or whether he was simply trying to intimidate them in turn so that they would let him go without any further questions.

"As I said," Emily carried on regardless, "we have questions for you. Like,"

"Like where have all the students gone?"

"And why does no one talk about it?"

"And what's happened to John?"

"And how come you're coaching mind frisbi when you're so bad at it yourself," said Jimmy. The questions had tumbled out of the mouths of Emily and Jimmy jointly one on top of the other in a confused assortment of inquisition. "That last one," he said towards Emily, "can probably wait, still I do wonder, I really do," he added to Gerald as he tightened his grip around his arm.

"Why should I tell you? Even if I did know the answers," Gerald added quickly, covering himself from any further accusations of hiding information.

"Because I have your arm," said Jimmy, flexing his muscles so that he raised Gerald's arm painfully, "and I'm thinking you would like it to stay with you when we let you go and not be separated from it."

"Mr. Cowan," the voice came from outside. "Miss Lee. I wonder whether I might have a word."

Jimmy and Emily turned to look towards the voice and realized that it was coming from President Dreyfus.

"Gerald," he continued, "you may go. Follow this way please," he said to Jimmy and Emily as he began to lead them down the corridor towards his presidential office. Gerald rubbed his arm where Jimmy had been holding it and as Jimmy and Emily looked back towards him, while they followed President Dreyfus, he mouthed the word "disappearing" to them, smirked, and skipped off down the corridor.

"You need not say anything," President Dreyfus said as they carried on towards his office, "all will be made clear momentarily."

Jimmy and Emily were wondering what exactly "all being made clear" would mean in this instance, and were thinking how many other students who had disappeared had followed the same route to the president's office, what would happen to them there, would they be interrogated, taken to a Cognitive Prison, even…robotomized. Jimmy and Emily were passing thought pad terminal after terminal as they walked down the corridor so they dared not think along such lines for long, trying to keep their ideas hidden from observation, but as they walked they reached a hand out to each other and briefly their fingers touched to comfort one another. Jimmy thought of making a run for it, but as he turned around to scan for options he realized that following behind him and Emily were a couple of other teachers, and even, he realized with a gulp, Ms. Meadows in her Cognitive Police uniform, bulging at every corner.

As they turned a corner, hands touching encouragingly as they feared for the worst, Emily noticed on a thought pad a strange set of words appear. "Stay Calm. Say nothing. Think nothing. Help is at hand." She did not have time to point it out to Jimmy, and did not want to alert those following to the message, but she

squeezed Jimmy's hand as if to say "everything will be okay."
He squeezed back as if to say, "yeah maybe...or maybe not...
but we've got to keep our spirits up, you know." He shrugged his
shoulders a little at the same time, as if he was resigning himself
to his fate. As they carried on walking, Emily noticed that
another thought pad quickly appeared with a message, "Touch
next thought pad. Make sure your hands are connected as you
do." Emily's heart beat faster. Perhaps help really was close. She
was not sure how that could possibly be true, but she dared to
hope a little.

There were no terminals, at least obvious thought pads, for
connecting to the Webispace for a few more steps down the
corridor, and the large looming doors of the president's office
were nearing. They were oak paneled, carved with the symbols
of Gayle College. As they came closer Emily was able to make
out once again the well-known crest, a picture of a man who had
recently been chained to a rock, wrestling himself free and shaking
his fist at heaven, and underneath the motto, *Imatatio Promethei*.

The president turned around to look at them, as he touched
the rock and the oak doors swung open immediately and slowly.
Before them was revealed an interior of large spaciousness,
crammed not (of course) with books but thought pads, terminals
and screens through which were still playing the activities of the
various students—probably, Emily thought, activities that were
going on right now, being transmitted, and watched, constantly
through the Webispace. She had not realized that all this was
channelled to the President's office.

They carried on walking as they did not seem to have much
choice, Emily still hoping against hope that the thought pad

message that "help is at hand" would somehow be proved right. The President smiled at them and gestured for them to go inside. They were three steps or so from the entrance when Emily noticed to her right, on the wall, a sign appear. It was a Christmas Rose. Above it was written: "Touch me." Without thinking further, and her hand still brushing against Jimmy's, she immediately reached out, touched the rose, and with a strange sensation like she imagined water must feel as it is swirled down a drain, she and Jimmy were twirled into another place.

It was dark. It was quiet.

"Splitting headache," said Jimmy, "is preferrable to that experience. Remind me never to hold hands with you again. Ouch!" he said as she pinched his hand, though he noticed she did not let go, stranded as they were (together) in the dark, and in the quiet.

"Where do you think we are?" Emily asked.

"No idea. It was you who touched that Christmas Rose thing. Who knew that my horticultural expertise would come in so useful?" Jimmy was once more chattering away bringing a light touch to the situation. "Still," he carried on in a slightly more serious tone, "I didn't like the look of that room. Creepy. I suspect we were about to disappear."

"On the other hand," said Emily, "I think we just did disappear. Not sure what that means, not sure where we are now, but I know we're not where we were. Perhaps everyone else thinks we've disappeared too now."

This was an uncomfortable thought. In the dark, and the silence, they both reflected on it for a moment. If they had known that John had been here before it would have greatly eased their concerns, but all they knew was that they were somewhere where they could see nothing and hear nothing. They could not even distinguish the hands that still touched one another.

"I don't mind holding your hand and all," said Jimmy, "but one day we might need to stop being Siamese twins. Perhaps not right yet," he added, realizing that in the dark if he let go he would not be able to pick out where Emily was at all, if he could not see the hand that touched hers.

"Twins," said Emily, thoughtfully.

"At any rate," said Jimmy, "This must be what it's like before you are born. I wonder where the exit is, or when we're going to suddenly experience some contractions."

"I'm not sure I like that metaphor," said Emily wincing a little in the dark. "Though I know what you mean. There's no Webispace. No light."

"Just us and our thoughts."

They were quiet again, in the dark silky silence. Neither Jimmy nor Emily afterwards could remember exactly how long this had carried on. Unlike John they had not thought they needed to make any progress, perhaps because they were there together they felt less desperate immediately to find an exit. They stood side by side, and after some further conversation reflecting on what they thought was a near escape from the Cognitive Police, they said nothing, and nothing was said for some time. Their thoughts were not being read by each other, nor by anyone else, and as John experienced before they individually began to recognize ideas, pictures, words, shapes in their own heads generated by themselves internally, not forced from outside into their minds. They were thinking, depicting, being. Their sense of self, twinned together, attached by their hands, was gradually regrowing chrysalid like; they were not yet butterflies but they were no longer quite worms either.

A hand grabbed from behind at both Emily and Jimmy at the same time. "Follow me," someone said, and in single file, Emily's arm now resting on Jimmy's shoulder, they followed the leader slowly, inchingly, scraping their shoes along the floor and gradually working their way towards whatever destination lay before them.

A candle flared with light, and the leader lit other candles around the walls of the room. It was not the Underground chamber where John had been taken, and there were not twelve chairs facing a fire, though another fire was there which now was lit. Instead of the twelve members of the Underground, in their hooded cloaks, Emily quickly realized that the room—which obviously until a moment before their arrival had not been lit— was buzzing with activity, as well as familiar faces. There was John Broadus looking towards them with a big, if somewhat dirty, grin on his face. There, Emily realized, was Faith Felicity too. There were several other of the students who she thought had disappeared.

"Where are we?" she asked one of the hooded figures who had led them here.

He, she thought it was he by the sound of his voice, replied, "We have brought you to the training center for the Underground. You are safe. For a while. There is no electricity, no Webispace. You may think as you like, speak as you like. But you have much work to be done. For now, I and my friend here," he indicated the other hooded figure who had guided Jimmy from behind, "will leave you to be reunited with your fellow students."

"It's okay," said John racing up to greet them. "I'm not sure entirely what's going on but they are training us to think. To be able to mount a counter initiative against Gayle College and its ways." He did not say anything about the wider ambition he had heard from the Underground twelve of him helping retake New Angle Land as a whole; it seemed presumptuous, too early, and there were many other, happy, things on his mind.

"We're learning brilliant stuff," said Faith Felicity coming over to greet them as well.

Emily looked around the room. There were four or five other students as well as Faith and John. "Where are all the rest?" she asked. "There have been far more disappearances from Gayle College than just this number."

"They didn't get to them all in time," said John. "As you can tell from your experience it is a close run thing to be able to evacuate—that's the word they use—someone when they have become under suspicion of being epistemic."

"What happened to the others then?" said Jimmy, also concerned.

"We don't know for sure, and they haven't told us if they know or not," said Faith. "We think…" her voice trailed off.

"We think they have been taken by the Cognitive Police and either put in prison or perhaps…worse."

"You mean robotomized," said Jimmy. No one said anything.

"Anyway," said John changing the subject, as there was nothing he could do about that at least for the moment, "even those who have been wrongly thrown into Cognitive Prison some of them escaped, and not all of them were…recaptured." He explained what he had seen about the Cognitive Prison escape to Faith.

"How did they get out?" asked Faith

"I think that was something they arranged too," said John. "I think some of the Underground Twelve have figured out a way to penetrate the Webispace mentally unobserved if only very briefly, as you saw with your evacuation. The same happened with me. Of course," John said, "such penetration of the Webispace is extremely difficult and risky and I don't think even many of the Underground Twelve have managed it."

"Apparently John can do it without trying," said Faith looking at Emily with a smile.

"That's not quite true," said John, "they think," he wasn't quite sure how to say this, "that I have some unusual natural abilities, but I have to learn to control them before I can be of much use. Apparently I have to learn to think."

"I always said that of you, mate," said Jimmy.

"What do we do now?" Dreyfus wondered out loud, as he slumped into his seat behind the wide expanse of his presidential desk. None of the other teachers had followed him into the office once they had realized that Jimmy and Emily had somehow been evacuated; he was alone except for Ms. Meadows.

"Do?" she said pacing up and down in front of the desk, walking across the expensive carpet embossed with the Gayle College crest and motto, "Do? *We* do nothing." She touched her hand to the thought pad on the edge of the president's desk and was immediately mentally transported to stand in front of a hooded, wheelchair-bound figure, sitting alone in the Council room beneath the great central Cathedral.

There was an exchange of mental pictures from Ms. Meadows to the Chair of the Council, while he observed and mentally requested the president to transmit as well. Having received all the information, the Chair, his face shrouded by his hood, put his finger tips to his lips and thought a reply.

"We must bring up our program. Ms. Meadows, I want them found. Dr. Dreyfus, weed out the epistemic students from your midst. We can have no more rotten apples."

"But will that be enough?" said Ms. Meadows.

"For the rest," said the Chair, "leave it to me."

John had lain down for a break before he was brought into his next stage of training. So far he had been asked to clear his mind of mental projections from the Webispace and learn to think his own thoughts. Faith had been particularly adept at understanding how information fitted together into a whole, and was not only a matter of experience in a flood of sensations but had a unity to it. John had been listening and learning from her account of her mental growth disconnected from the Webispace. But for John they wanted to try to see if they could replicate his experiences in the Webispace, his unknowing ability to move through the Webispace and observe and make connections that only the most trained of the Underground Twelve could do, and see if they could help him harness that ability for the Underground.

"There are many others," one of the hooded leaders had explained to him, "who seek our help, or would benefit from it if we could regularly make contact with them, if we could release them from being constantly spied on by the Walkers. We have this room," the speaker explained as he led John further in and further up, "where there is a single Webispace portal, usually disconnected, which we use for very brief forays into the Webispace so that we can evacuate individuals like yourself."

Their journey to this room took some time, as they walked slowly up a winding corridor into the gloom, carrying a candle each. As they entered John noticed that the candle shone on a sign attached to the door which read "Cappadocia." Inside, John was asked to take a seat on a wooden bench, straddle it, and be ready to place his hand on what looked like an extremely basic thought pad.

"We take this position so that we are not comfortable physically which helps us to prevent ourselves from becoming too comfortable mentally. It is also easier," the speaker went on "for someone else to take over from the other side of the bench." He sat down facing John. "Right, remember what you have learnt. Do not receive. Project, but be wary *what* you project. You must only project thoughts about mind frisbi, not Gayle College, not your friends, certainly not the Underground, or your encounters here. Only mind frisbi games. Everything else will be monitored. Do you understand?" John nodded. "Well, let us begin. Place your hand on the thought pad."

John touched the pad and once more the familiar feeling of being mentally connected to the Webispace began. It had been several days, at least, since he had last connected like this, so it felt strange to be back in the stream of information. As this portal was so ancient, it was an effort to make connection, but he imagined that was all part of the reason as well, to make it hard work so that the person connected did not become too comfortable, or passive, but continued to project thoughts from within, controlled thoughts, rather than simply receive what was projected through the Webispace into their minds. It was also not at the center of the Webispace zones, so it was almost as if he had to reenter from below into the mainstream.

"Careful," the voice of the hooded figure opposite was briefly mentally projected into his mind as he touched the thought pad himself for a moment too, "you are about to enter the central aspects of the Webispace, so far you have been a long way from where most Walkers travel, but in a moment you will be in the thorough fare of the traffic of the Webispace. Remember: control, think for yourself, project, don't simply receive."

John nodded once more, and his journey continued back into the main route of the Webispace. He was surrounded by a million suggestions and options, competing for his mind's attention, he ignored them concentrating on actively contributing through his general thoughts about mind frisbi. So far, so good. The hooded figure opposite him smiled encouragingly.

Suddenly, John felt as if a wind like a tornado gathered him up, spun him round, took him from where he had been meandering along unconcernedly, and dumped him into a totally different part of the Webispace. John was too shocked to notice what the hooded member of the Underground opposite was doing, whether he had realized what had taken place, or was trying to rectify it. John's heart was still beating fast from the sudden change of pace, and his mind was mentally reeling from the feeling of being zipped up like a speck of dust by a vacuum cleaner and deposited once the wind reversed direction somewhere else. Or like being sucked under water at the base of a rushing water fall, turned around several times, and then spat out again further down the river. It was not his doing, at least it did not feel like it was, and he was not sure he liked it—did not like it at all.

As John breathed for a moment, the spinning and rotating had stopped and he was stable once more, he observed where he was. He was not at the super secure Cognitive Crime prison that he had unwittingly visited before, now he was in a community, but it was a community different from most parts of New Angle Land. He had seen communities like this before in the Webispace news, it was a quarantine community of those who had caught the Contagion or become epistemic. They called it a gated secure community for those at risk; the tag line advertizing them was "for us...and for them," suggesting that the purpose was not just seclusion of risky individuals from the wider society but also curing those individuals so that they could reenter society at the right moment. John had never heard of anyone reentering.

Unlike the pictures that were used to advertize, the gated community did not appear pristine with flowers and smiling Cognitive Police waving at the inhabitants. It was surrounded with barbed wire, guarded by dogs, and the Cognitive Police were armed and dangerous. Inside, John observed as he was mentally drawn further in, was line after line of shoddy, tiny, houses, interspersed with high rise grubby concrete blocks with broken windows, and entrance way doors with graffiti on them, and hanging off their hinges. "Not exactly idyllic," John thought, and then stopped himself, remembering how important it was that he not be discovered as he was at this moment connected to the Underground portal.

As John watched, so far unobserved he believed, an extra group of Cognitive Police arrived at the gate. They were followed by a large truck, eighteen wheels, black. They showed their papers to the Cognitive Police person on duty, were waved inside and began to round up the residents. They went from house to house, guns out, apartment building to apartment building, dragging out men, women, and children. Even a dog or two was cuffed across the face as they protested; one was shot, whimpering as it died.

The people were herded into line, and one by one they went up a ramp into the enormous truck. On the other side they came out, unsmiling, unprotesting, vacant look in their eyes, and were taken off to be clothed in the uniform of lower grade workers in the Webispace call centers. For a moment John mentally was given a glimpse of what was going on inside. Minds were attached directly to thought pads, heads forced down so that their foreheads (not their hands) touched their pads, a thought pad was enveloped from behind, a button was pressed, and the victims shuddered, spittle frothed, and in a few moments it was over. John was so shocked he physically wrenched his hand from the thought pad.

He stared at the hooded figure opposite him who obviously had no idea what John had just seen. "We must stop them," said John. "Now. There can be no more delay. Take me back to the Underground Twelve chamber. We must act."

Chapter Eleven

NEW BEGINNING

"It will end poorly," said the main speaker standing up as he considered.

John and Jimmy and Emily had been brought immediately into the late night gathering of the Underground Twelve, flickering candlelight on the walls and a fire glowing warmly in the grate.

"If you act now, you might prevent it from happening but you may fail and then our opportunity will be gone."

There were several parts of this statement that John did not understand. "What do you mean 'might prevent it from happening'? What I saw is taking place now."

"What you saw," said the main speaker, passing lightly from chair to chair of the Underground Twelve as he talked, "is what will happen soon, no doubt, but it is only the beginning of a wider program of robotomization that the Council Chair is planning.

You have seen the seed that is planted, the oak tree is yet to grow. If you act now you might stop one or two of these further developments, but you are more likely to fail, and then the wider program will continue and our carefully developed plan to stop it from taking place, and retake New Angle Land, will be gone."

"There's something else I don't get," said John thinking, "what do you mean by saying 'if *you* act now'? I thought you were the Underground Twelve. I thought it was your job to act." There was a shuffling of feet as John said this, and the main speaker turned his shadowed face towards him so that once again John caught a glimpse of an outline of a face that—for a moment, he was not quite sure—he thought he recognized.

"So it is," the speaker said consolingly, "so it is…and yet at this moment, your abilities, and your insight, mean there is something that you could do that no one else can."

"Stop!" said a female voice from the semi-circle of the Underground Twelve. "I will not have him know anymore."

"Not yet at least," came another, gruffer, male voice, the same voice John thought that had spoken against the main direction of the Underground Twelve on the first evening that he had been presented.

"You see, John," said the main speaker quietly, "we are not all agreed. And yet we are all aware that you could, perhaps, do something now that no one else could do. At the same time we all know it is a risk, a risk for you, your friends, and…"

"And for the whole plan," said the female voice.

"Indeed," continued the speaker. "So our advice is that you do nothing. Not yet."

"What about those people I saw? I can't just leave them to their fate!" John replied, becoming more agitated at the passivity of this Underground resistance.

"There is always collateral damage," said the gruff voice, "better them than all of us, better we sacrifice some blood now for the greater good."

"You understand," said the main speaker, "don't you John? We feel the same as you but we must keep the wider picture. So, as I say…"

"As he says," interrupted the female voice, "Do nothing."

"Carry on your training. You still have a lot to learn, my boy," said the gruff male voice.

"Nothing," said John, "is the one thing I cannot do."

"Nice going," said Jimmy, as they trudged along slowly, arm on shoulder, one in front of the other up the dark pathway back towards ground level. "As soon as we get some friends you annoy them. Just as I was getting cozy and comfortable down there, candlelights, hard rock, old wooden chairs—home away from home I say."

John could not quite decide whether Jimmy was frustrated that they were leaving, pleased that they were leaving, or simply enjoying the chance to crack a few jokey ironical comments as they walked together out of reach of any connection to the Webispace.

"It's not like they gave you the royal goodbye is it? Keep on going, they said, it's easy just follow the path until you come to a dead end, they said, it'll be dark, they said, but you're used to that now. It makes me almost wish," he muttered finally under his breath, "for that horrible whooshing feeling we had when we transported down here first of all, better than a slow march into something as black as Gerald Hawthorne's underarm pit."

"Oh come on," said Emily, "it's not as bad as all that. It could be Ms. Meadows' underarm pit."

"Now don't get disgusting," Jimmy said as he shuffled forward, "you won't be able to see if I vomit but you'll still feel it."

Emily was in the middle of the line, Jimmy behind her, and John leading the way at the head. After what seemed like forever, so long that Jimmy had stopped talking and Emily had stopped trying to calm him down, and there was once more silence, dark, silky silence, John's right foot hit against a wall. They were walking slowly, shuffling really, so it was not painful for John but as he reached out his hand and touched the wall he realized that they had come to the end of the path.

"This is it," said John. "We've arrived."

"By 'arrived' I hope you mean 'we're about to get out of here' because if this is your idea of 'arrival' then I can tell you more what my idea is…it begins," mused Jimmy, "with ice cream, beaches, swimming pools, and it ends with massages from beautiful women wearing…*Oi!*" said Jimmy as Emily shoved him in the stomach before he could continue. "Alright, alright mind back on the here and now. There was better though, 'arrived' I tell you, huh!"

"Okay," said John, "they told me that when we arrived while we prepared for exit…" As John said this water sprayed on them all from above, warm it was true, but sharp and hard and significantly shocking as it was so unexpected. It was like being showered from every direction at once, while wearing your day clothes, and without any warning. In fact that was exactly what it was, except the water also contained soap.

"They told me," John's muffled surprised voice shouted back at the other two, "that being prepared for exit might not be quite what we had imagined."

"You don't say!" said Emily as her hair was drenched, and then soaped, and then drenched again.

They did not know it but being underground had covered their faces and their hands with dirt. But this exit shower was not just to clean them up so they looked presentable, it was to remove any possible microbe signs of their whereabouts so if they were caught the location of the Underground could not be discovered. John had the feeling that though they had seen the place where the Twelve met, and the training centre, there was much more to it that they had not yet been shown. It was all for safety, they had been assured, though they had no reason to be ready for a shower of warm soapy water spraying at them from every direction.

"We'll be clean," said Jimmy, "but I think people might notice that we look a little bit wet. Could be a bit of a giveaway in the middle of the day, if that's what it is, turning up drenched through and through with the sun shining, if that's what it's doing." Just as Jimmy said this, the water stopped. "Ah," he said, "I was beginning to feel like a fish having its tank cleaned. Whoa!" his voice shouted as now instead of water falling on them, and coming at them from every direction, warm air blew at them, hard, almost painful. It was so strong it was a little difficult to breathe. "I…ALWAYS…" shouted Jimmy above the noise when he managed to catch a breath, "WANTED…TO…BLOW DRY…MY   HAIR…BUT   I…NEVER…THOUGHT… THAT WOULD…MEAN…THIS!" he concluded as the wind stopped, and felt around his body and clothes to notice that they were as dry as sandpaper. "Good thing I wasn't wearing my Sunday best," he added finally.

Emily was trying desperately to rearrange her hair, assuming it would be sticking up on end and coming out crazily at every angle. Actually, if she had been able to see, her hair had been nearly perfectly styled, as the air draft was intended to return them to their appearance before their time underground. In fact, they all looked about as good as they ever had.

"Now," said John, "they said that in a moment we'll be reversed. I suppose that means that we'll be sucked back up the way we came."

"How does that work anyway?" said Emily, "I thought the Webispace could only move you mentally."

"I don't think it's exactly the Webispace," said John, "I heard them call it the 'transportal'. It's connected, very temporarily, to the Webispace, it takes massive amounts of power, and the Underground twelve have designed it so they can move around actually physically without being detected by the Webispace Walkers. One of the reasons they think I am…"

"Special," said Jimmy smiling in the darkness and prodding John in the ribs as he stood ahead of him

"Whatever," said John, "…Unusual, I suppose…is that they think my experiences in the Webispace when I seem to go places and see things might be actually me…going places and seeing things…I might actually be transporting through the Webispace. No one's done that before. They're not sure, mind, and I can't do it reliably yet. That's why…"

"That's why we're standing here liked baked prunes waiting for our exit," said Jimmy with a laugh.

Without warning, each of them maintaining contact as they had been told, they were twirled through the air, sucked up and out, reversed, like water instead of being drained away coming back up the drain, like someone coming out of a whirlpool at the bottom of a water fall and sliding back up the water to the calm water at the top.

"Fun," said Jimmy, as they stood together, no longer touching, but looking around at where they had been reversed to. "Can't wait to do that again. Almost as much fun as a good kick in the head, upside down, under water, three times over, by your best friend, while you are wearing underpants and all your class is watching. Fun, great fun, can't wait to be transported again, can't wait." He patted his body up and down, making sure all the limbs were still attached. "You look good," he said glancing at Emily, whose hair seemed to have been perfectly coiffured by the experience.

"Well, thank you Mr. Cowan," Emily gave a little ironic curtsy.

They had landed at the footsteps to the front of Gayle College. It felt like a different life when John had turned up on those steps for his first day at the College, when his parents had embarrassingly bid him farewell. He remembered seeing all the mind frisbis zipping around the entrance that day, and all the students milling around, trying to catch each other's eyes, third years looking to impress second years, second years looking to impress first years, first years trying hard not to appear as nervous as they felt. Now all was empty.

The Underground Twelve had explained to them that transportal was only possible through the most advanced of thought pads, as it required massive amounts of energy. That was why they had had to be transported through next generation A+ pads or official pads, as they had been transported from right outside the President's office, or down in the subway near a Cognitive Police enclave. It was not possible to just do it anywhere, and they had been transported to within a few metres of the front Gate of the College because there was a thought pad that was used by all the students, and parents, and was one of the most advanced of its kind. The Underground had also warned them that the surge of energy would set off alarm systems in the Webispace, might alert the Cognitive Police, and once they had arrived they should quickly move on before they were spotted.

"Come on," said John, "We need to keep going." They ran up the steps, into the quad, and noticed as they did so that some

Cognitive Police vehicles descended from the airway above and began to prowl around to see what might have taken place. They were, as yet, though, unnoticed.

"Why, again, remind me, did we come back here?" said Emily, "I thought that the robotomization was taking place in the quarantine areas not at the college."

"I just think it all connects here," said John, "I don't know why," he added as he noticed the incredulous look on Jimmy and Emily's face as they glanced at each other. "I just feel this is the right place to go, and the Underground twelve seemed to think I might have a good intuition about it."

"These are the people who just soaked us and blow dried us, right?" said Jimmy, "Good to know we're getting our advice from the highest sources." Emily gave him a playful punch on the arm. "Ow! Just saying that's all."

"The point is," continued Emily smiling, "That John thinks this is where we need to be, and that's good enough for us, isn't it Jimmy. Okay, John, here we are, what now?"

John did not like to admit it but he was really not quite sure. It felt right being here, somehow there was a 'node' of connections to this point, and if he could cut that connection then he felt that the other events he had witnessed would also be cut, or at least delayed for now.

"This way," said John, following his instincts.

They all knew that soon enough they would be recognized. Indeed as they took a turn into the corridor that led to the classrooms of

Gayle College, it was John H. Johnson who spotted them first.

He looked at them and stopped. His eyes glanced around him. "Where did you come from? Where have you been? Every time someone goes we are told not to ask but that they will return once they are feeling better. Are you feeling better?" His face took on an almost comically concerned expression.

"Much better, H." said Jimmy.

"Where are you going?" H. asked as they kept on walking past him, following John.

"Follow us and find out," said John, not sure why he said this but sure it was the right thing to do. Soon enough John, Emily and Jimmy had a little crowd of students following them down the corridors, bemused, unsure where they were going, where John and Emily and Jimmy had been, or what was about to happen.

Some were there out of genuine concern, others were there because any old excuse would do instead of homework, some were there because everyone else was there. Labelle Malchance was in this last category as she walked along next to Emily, trying to make the most of being in the limelight, or at least next to someone who was at that moment the focus of attention. She twirled her long blond hair, batted her eyelashes at the boys, and minced along, short steps, her legs springing back and forwards like well oiled pistons. Jimmy tried to go back a bit towards her, nearer to Emily and so nearer to Labelle, but each time he attempted to move closer he was given a little shove in between his shoulder blades by Emily keeping him ahead of the crowd.

"Where are we going?" said Emily to John as they kept on walking.

"I thought we were meant to be doing this *quietly*," said Jimmy, "whatever it is that we are doing."

"The time for secrecy is over," said John.

He kept on walking down the corridors, turning this way and that, with a growing crowd of noisy students behind him, increasingly certain of what he must do. They arrived at the impressive oak doors of the president's office. The crest stared back at them intimidatingly: *Imatatio Promethei.*

"Time," said John, reaching out his hand to touch the crest, "to imitate something else."

The doors swung open at his touch, and the crowd behind John craned to peer inside to see what was going on—most of them had never been in the president's office before, and John had only seen it through one of his Webispace episodes, whatever that meant. It was, though, exactly as he had observed, the crest on the carpet, the large expansive wooden desk, the screens constantly depicting all the activity of the Webispace recording students actions, except for the corridors down which they had walked which were, John realized, inexplicitly showing no action at all, incorrectly recording, failing to have warned the president of the approach of the students. John was not sure how that had happened. He wondered whether the Underground Twelve, despite their hesitancy about his presumptive action, were nonetheless lending their help.

The president, Gary E. Dreyfus, sat at his desk, opposite stood Ms. Meadows, large, whale-like, blubbery, puffy eyed, and momentarily shocked by the entrance of John, Jimmy, and Emily, and the crowd of students behind. The president said nothing. Ms. Meadows however quickly recovered her poise.

"How DARE you," she screeched, "barge in here like this unannounced to the president's office! We are having an important meeting. You all," she glared around at the students, raising her torso a little as she stood before them, emphasizing her police uniform, "need to go back to whatever it is you are meant to be doing at this hour, or else," she carried on quieter, having managed to gain their attention, "there will be *consequences.*"

The last word was spat out, not loudly, but sinisterly, snake-like, where each 's' sound was emphasized and elongated. Emily and Jimmy took a step back, and some of the students behind them actually physically hid behind each other, trying to avoid Ms. Meadows' gaze, hoping that they had not been noticed.

"The only consequences," John said levelly, realizing that however nervous he felt inside he would have to go through with this now he had started, "are going to be for you."

At this he reached forward, suddenly, quickly, without hesitation, to the thought pad at the center of the president's desk, and was immediately connected to the Webispace.

His training in the Underground had not been for nothing, for now he was able to control what parts of the information he had in his mind he transmitted, a technique that was rare, and was assumed by most of New Angle Land authorities to be, practically speaking, impossible, especially as most did not even try, thinking that the Webispace was only for receiving information, not for recording the thoughts of those connected as well.

John carefully selected the information he wished to transmit from his mind. He found the largest, most successful, and famous news cast organization on the Webispace, Central New Angleland News (CNAN), and broadcast to them, picture after picture of Ms. Meadows, intimidating students at the elite famous Gayle College, arresting John for no reason when he had not been speeding, using a mind probe on Jimmy and Emily. Ms. Meadows' large, expansive, Police uniformed body, was accompanied with each mental picture transmitted, and as it was sent to CNAN newscast, coming directly from John's mind, it was transmitted, unedited, though all the Webispace news portals, and conversations, all the way up to the highest levels of government. Ms. Meadows attempted physically to stop John from transmitting through the Webispace, but Jimmy, noticing finally what John was doing, restrained her as he had Gerald Hawthorne. "You're big," said Jimmy as she wrestled vainly against his muscular physique, "but you're not strong."

No doubt the secretive Council were alerted to this sudden transmittal of information about Ms. Meadows around the Webispace, but with the notional government now exposed to the information, and everyone else aware, they could take no action. Once John disconnected, a Webispace newscast from the chief of police of New Angle Land formed on every screen in the president's office. All the students could see, and they craned around the doors to make sure that they did not miss anything.

"Reports have been received regarding inappropriate activity by Ms. Meadows of the Cognitive Police in the Gayle College district. As of this moment her authority is removed pending a full investigation. Cognitive Police personnel are being sent as I speak to collect Ms. Meadows for further questioning."

As the Webispace newscast finished, and returned to the normal screens showing entertainment, news, and various parts of Gayle College, Ms. Meadows face shifted from triumph, as she looked at John hungrily, to horror as she scanned the faces of the students. "President Dreyfus, you know…!"

"Stop, Ms. Meadows. You are under investigation."

Before he finished, Cognitive Police arrived within moments and took Ms. Meadows away. The students cheered. John and Emily hugged. "Steady on there mate," said Jimmy, as he looked around furtively for Labelle Malchance hoping for a hug from her, but was disappointed to notice that she was giving John H. Johnson a playful hug instead. "No accounting for taste," he said sulkily.

Emily and Jimmy and John were back in their alcove. "Do you think we need to meet here anymore?" Emily asked John.

"I don't know," said John, "but I think it's safer if we do for now. Perhaps it's not necessary."

"Perhaps it is though," said Jimmy, sounding uncharacteristically meaningful. "You can never tell," he added, "and anyway that President Dreyfus is still in place."

"What's happened to all those quarantine areas?" asked Emily.

"I think," said John, "the Council and that Chair person in the wheelchair have had to back off from their plans…for now… There's been too much attention given to illicit activity among the police once Ms. Meadows was exposed. Everyone is on the lookout for the moment. They can't do anything at this point."

"So it worked," said Emily.

"Yes," said John, "at least…"

"At least" continued Jimmy, "so far."

The last class of the semester before summer holidays arrived. It was more *Lessons in Logical Positivity*, taken by Professor E.C. White. His voice droned on and on, as the sounds of summer creeped in through the windows to the classroom. Their hands were attached to the thought pads, but their minds kept on thinking of what the summer would bring, how many parties they could go to, how much swimming they could get done. Every time they drifted off in this way, E.C. White would scream inside their heads. "Mr. *Cowman*," he shouted mentally to Jimmy, "back to the classroom, if you please!" Jimmy shook himself awake and tried without a great deal of success to concentrate on the meandering paths of logical positivity.

At the end of the class, E.C. White asked John to stay behind. "Watch out," said Emily, "you know what could happen around here."

"Yeah," said Jimmy, "don't get too close he has terrible bad breath." Emily looked at him, "Or at any rate so I hear."

John walked to the front of the class while E.C. White bent down and unlocked a draw in his desk. He brought out a shiny, brand new, next generation thought pad.

"That's the A+," said John.

"Yes Mr. Broadus, it is. And now it's yours. Well done. Use it carefully, Mr. Broadus. You have passed the first test, but some of us know more than you think we do."

John ignored Professor White's half hearted gift as he ran out of the room to catch up with Jimmy and Emily who were making their way to the quad, the central court area of Gayle College. Mind frisbi were lazily passing from student to student as they pretended to be interested in their studies, but were really either dozing, talking, or simply pruning themselves in front of each other. Jimmy and Emily and John sat down on the steps leading down to the quad and watched with smiles on their faces. "So ends the first year," said John.

The last day had arrived. John next to Jimmy and Emily in their usual place for breakfast. They were waiting to be picked up by their parents—a source of ongoing grievance for the students, who, despite the New Angle Land laws, wished that they did not always have to be collected but could make their own way back home. John in particular was not looking forward to seeing his parents. He could not imagine what his mother would say to him. Something like, "remember when you get home we have lots of chores for you to do," he expected. As John sat down he noticed a parcel, brown paper parcel, was at his place.

"What's that?" said John, "last time I opened one of these a lot of bad things happened really fast. Did you put it there?" he looked suspiciously at Jimmy, and then Emily, wondering if they were playing him some kind of prank, but both of them shook their heads, and carried on eating.

"We are wondering the same, mate," said Jimmy.

"Is it for me?" said John

"Didn't we go through this last time?" said Jimmy, "it's at your place, not mine or hers, and it says on the outside 'for John Broadus only.' I think that's a bit of a giveaway."

John silently started to eat. "I'll open it later," he said.

After breakfast John took the parcel back up to his room, stood in the middle of the room so he was least likely to be connected to the Webispace, and started to unwrap the parcel. After a short while brown paper from the parcel was lying at his feet. A card fell out of the parcel. It said, "the truth will set you free."

"I thought I'd already found the truth," thought John to himself as he observed the card, and then placed it carefully in his pocket for further consideration later. "Perhaps there's more to come," he said out loud this time.

He looked at what was in the parcel. It was a book. This one was old, tatty, worn. "At least you could have given me a *new* book," he said out loud again, not sure why he was saying this rather than just thinking it.

He opened up the book. The first few pages were blank. He turned to the first printed page. He started to read, "In the beginning," it read, "God…"